D1448497

CUPCAKES AND COFFEE

REBECCA STONE

SilverWood

Published in 2014 by SilverWood Books

SilverWood Books Ltd
30 Queen Charlotte Street, Bristol, BS1 4HJ
www.silverwoodbooks.co.uk

ISBN 978-1-78132-335-9 (paperback)
ISBN 978-1-78132-336-6 (ebook)

British Library Cataloguing in Publication Data
A CIP catalogue record for this book is available from
the British Library

Set in Sabon by SilverWood Books
Printed on responsibly sourced paper

Friday 31st December, 2010

Voices on 17th Street began to cheer and shouts of 'Happy New Year' rang out from various bars on Valencia, and at that exact moment the man in my bed had an orgasm. I'd love to tell you that my technique had perfectly timed his explosion of ecstasy with the distant sound of fireworks but, in all honesty, it was a total fluke. However, the brilliance of the moment made me laugh out loud, which isn't the best thing to do at a moment like that. He looked at me slightly confused.

'Happy New Year,' I said as if presenting him with the next best thing on The Shopping Channel and kissed him.

'Was that New Year's?'

'Yep and that was a great way to start it.' I immediately wished I'd said something less tacky.

There is a superstition that if you don't have sex on New Year's Eve with your partner then the relationship will suffer from a drought for the rest of the year. This isn't my partner, so I don't think it counts, but I am going to make it count because my love life has been a dryer than the Sahara recently.

This marks a turning point for me; I am always nostalgic on New Year's Eve. I like looking back and weighing up whether I am doing better this year than last, or any other year for that matter. It does, however, mean I drive myself really hard to make each year better than the last. Yet I realise that life isn't linear, it is at best repetitive circles. Most of us like to think we are smart and progressive; we just can fix our problems and enjoy a better and better life. Well that's me anyway, always looking for the next up.

Now this young man could be classed as a massive up. I'm thirty-nine on the cusp of turning forty and he has to be in his early twenties. In fact, he's so young that when I asked him how old he was he said, 'Twenty, no twenty-one,' because his birthday is in a few days' time. The older you get the more you hang on to the last few days of the age you are. He's so young, he could still say things like 'I'm twenty and three-quarters.' Old Father Time, who has just vanished off for another year, would envy him.

We met in the 500 Club about thirty minutes ago. He was sitting at the bar alone, which I thought was odd on New Year's Eve. It's fine if you're at home watching a pre-recorded Jules Holland show, as those celebs wouldn't really abandon their families over the holidays. Then you can be alone, but not in a bar. So, I decided to check on him.

There was a small amount of space next to him so I slid my way in and promptly ignored him, focusing on the bar staff and getting served, which wasn't as interesting to me as him. I hadn't even noticed how cute he was at this point. I can't even remember what he said to me. I don't even know if I heard him. All I can remember is how he fixed me with his blue eyes and turned me into a flirtatious vixen with pushed-out breasts. The one thing I do remember him saying stopped my breath and changed the game plan for the evening.

'You are so unbelievably sexy, I could take you home right now.'

'Really?' I said, trying to sound coy and flirtatious but I think he could hear my shock.

He laughed, 'Yes really.'

Blood rushed around my body, making me feel slightly giddy and hot. I moved towards him and stopped close to his face, as if I were setting him a dare – a dare that would reveal that he was joking. He countered my dare with eyes that moved from my eyes to my lips then back to my eyes as he moved forward for a kiss. I pressed my lips onto his, his beard felt really soft, and when he kissed me back it was as if he were greeting a much-missed old lover – passionate, connected and real. It was that quick.

Two or perhaps three sentences before that moment, part of me was struggling with the concept of taking him home. That's not what 'nice' women are supposed to do after all. We are meant to have dinner bought for us, go on a number of dates and when he has climbed up the tower on a plait of our hair, dealt with dwarves and killed a dragon, then and only then are we allowed to give ourselves up for sex. We have to make them work for it.

The problem is, I like sex, and sometimes first-time sex is better with someone you DON'T know that well. In fact, it can be far better than sex with someone you have been in a long-term relationship with, when the desire has gone right out of it and the act has become an obligation. Women say 'no' to gain respect, but by not going with your heart, when your whole body is saying 'yes', you can miss out on so many of the beautiful moments in life. I didn't want to miss the chance of being with this beautiful man on New Year's Eve.

It's amazing what rushes through your mind in terms of logistics, everything from minty fresh breath to letting the dog out for a pee, and what to say to Nat, who I'd set out with that evening. Luckily Nat and I have an understanding when it comes to men. Well, I *had* an understanding. I was her handbag caddy for the dance floor, as she usually got all the guys.

She look confused when I handed her two bottles of Corona, but then she saw the look in my eyes, took a look behind me and said, 'Oh, my God, go now before *he* changes *his* mind.'

In the half a block that it took to get home, I felt like I had stolen him – from the bar, from seeing in New Year with whomever he had been with in the bar. There was a sexual adrenaline rush going on making me feel more confident than I really was. In my bedroom, I told him to take his clothes off in a dramatic way with my arm stretched out up the doorframe, and wait while I took the dog out for a pee. This was more of an act of cruelty, as the heating didn't work. If you can call it heating: it is a vent in the wall to let in cool air in the summer. I think it was attached to a hairdryer on the other end. Being British this isn't a problem for me, but my San Francisco flatmates (or roomies, as they refer to themselves) freeze. Standing outside I was getting cold in more ways than one and willed my dog to pee.

'Go on then do a tiddle,' I said trying not to sound anxious as otherwise she becomes concerned and then won't pee.

'*Do* a tiddle.' How perfect does a patch of grass have to smell to pee on it?

'Take a freakin' PISS!'

Finally she squatted and then I had to give her the last treat of the day when we got indoors. Without the treat she won't know it was the last pee of the night and ask to pee again.

When I came back into the room, he was standing by the bed semi-naked with his bottom half missing. In the half-light of the fairy lights strung around the bed, which I'd left on for the dog, I could see the contours of his body, with his erect cock holding up the bottom of his T-shirt like a curtain tie.

I moved to kiss him, tongues rubbing together, licking and sucking to make him fill up my mouth. I ran my fingers up the inside of his thigh, lightly grazing my nails over one of his balls until his whole body shuddered. Wrapping my hand around his cock, his tongue paused for a moment signalling his intense anticipation, as his focus moved momentarily from our kiss to my hand and then my fingers, which I started to slowly move up the silken skin of his penis to the head. Gratifyingly covered in pre-cum, I used it to make my hand wet before drawing him back and forth with my hand. His knees, now softened from my touch, buckled slightly and so allowed me to guide him gently towards the bed, where he surrendered with me on top of him. Hips in time, kissing urgently, we made love with only the smallest layers of the material between us – my tights and pants, being the difference between him being inside me.

Wet right through, he got to work removing his shirt then my clothes. Much easier just to hop off and do it myself, so I did. It's never how it is in the TV show *Grey's Anatomy* where clothes just vanish between one camera angle and the next. In first-time drunk sex, foreplay happens after. It's a good deal harder to cum when you're drunk. With this in mind, I handed a condom to him and lay next to him waiting while he put it on. Ready now, he moved his cold fingers over my hot wet clitoris while still lying beside me. I'm used to a guy jumping on top of me as soon as the condom is in place. I looked into his eyes as he touched me to see if he wanted me to move on top, but he just kept softly drawing circles with his fingers and holding my gaze as he moved on top, lining up his cock with the same hand and, with one push was inside me. My hands grasped and dug into his shoulders as it felt just that bit too much and my body had to open too quickly to get used to his size. He massaged my breasts with his still wet hand and muttered something that started with 'Amazing...' But I lost the rest of what he was saying.

I've noticed that guys over here are more vocal in bed than the British. Americans gasp, groan, growl and...talk. British men tend to be the more stoic, silent type, just giving a polite grunt at orgasm – to let you know they've come. I felt him start to orgasm, his whole body jerking as he thrust upwards. Unconscious of the words coming out of my mouth, as if it weren't me saying them, I heard myself saying, 'Oh God' and 'Yes' – tacky, yet totally appropriate for the intensity of feeling. The rest you already know, street cheers and me wishing him a Happy New Year.

He told me his name is Jax, (short for Jaxson, very American) and he works as a barista in a coffee and bakery shop downtown. He was in the bar with his cousin, who he's been staying with since he moved to San Francisco a few months back. He can't stay there much longer because his cousin's girlfriend doesn't want him around anymore, so now he's looking for a place of his own, but rents are really high in San Francisco and he hasn't found anywhere yet. He and his cousin just had a big argument, which is why he was sitting by himself in the club. He was mostly brought up by women, older sisters and his mom, and is going to visit them tomorrow for three weeks and taking an early flight back to Seattle.

All this he tells me with his arms wrapped round me while I nestle into his chest. From time to time I move my face so I can smell the scent of his neck. I have a thing about hip and collarbones, and both of his protrude nicely. I draw small circles around his hipbones over his soft skin as he speaks. He talks quietly like he is already aware of my flatmates without me having to tell him. The word 'Seattle' makes me sit up a bit. I have wanted to go to Seattle since I lived in London, when I used to spend every Thursday evening with my upstairs neighbour with bottle of wine, a takeaway and a box of tissues watching *Grey's Anatomy*. The shots over the city of the lit-up skyscrapers and the Space Needle make the place look amazing. Jax bursts that bubble when he tells me that the show is filmed in LA. I avoid asking him if he's ever met Kurt Cobain. After all, that would be *all* my Seattle connections used up and it's likely that he was in nappies when *Never Mind* came out. It would have been almost as bad as him asking me if I'd ever met Princess Diana!

I tell him about my life, or rather my past life, as I haven't really made a life for myself in San Francisco. About selling my house in London and using the money to launch my book in the US. How I'd come here as a student on an undergraduate degree and had just completed my last year. The programme now means that I have a work permit, albeit restricted to my field of study, so I am volunteering for a company greening-up the local independent coffee houses in the Bay Area, while continuing my London career as a love coach over Skype. How I was also a yoga teacher, but had given it up because yoga teachers are two-a-cent over here!

I feel tears well up a little when he tells me how impressed he is, and how much guts that must have taken. It feels like the first intimate moment I've had since I got here. The first time I don't feel obliged to sell myself to make a life. I bruise it off with my natural superwoman approach, but it did take guts and I'm not sure how much of those I have left.

'What's the book about?' he asks.

Oh sod, I start playing with the forelock of my hair. It's not that the irony of this has passed me by, a single woman who writes a book about love and sexual exploration.

'It's a kind of self-help sex guide.'

'That would be a book on masturbation!' He says, which makes me laugh.

'Right yes, no, it's a book about love and sex for people who are seeking a more intimate connection.'

'So does that make you a sexpert?'

'No, I believe in writing the book you need to read.'

He presses his lips against mine and opens my mouth with his tongue, before pulling back a little to say, 'You don't need to read it, I might, but I've never been much of a reader, I'm more into practical.'

His energy is more focused this time as he pushes his hand between my legs demandingly opening me up as if my body is weightless. My vagina, still engorged and wet from sex, now feels really sensitive, my clit growing hard instantly at the light strokes of his fingers. He moves in close to my ear and murmurs, 'You are so sexy.'

I can feel his warm breath on my breasts as he moves from licking and sucking one nipple then the other. The refrigerator-like coldness of the room makes my nipples even harder than they would have been from his tongue alone. Chills run over my body as he brushes me ever so slightly with the hair from his beard, his lips moving down my body with small kisses. Pausing with his mouth over my pussy, I wait for him to touch me. Caressing the back of his neck and of his hairline to encourage him to keep going, but still he doesn't move.

My clit starts to pulse as though it's trying to get longer to reach his mouth. Then with one flick of his tongue, he pinpoints the tip of ecstasy and sends shock waves right up through my body, like a pinball bouncing from one erogenous zone to another. His thumbs open my lips as he focuses his tongue movements on the right spot. My fingers are digging into the back of his neck, trying not distracting him, nor pushing him closer to me. Moving his middle finger inside me, he massages my G-spot as he speeds up the intensity of his tongue on my clit.

Most women know that there is a strong link between the opening of her heart and her orgasm. So, as I feel the waves of pleasure driving me towards orgasm, fear keeps stopping me from submitting to the multitude of emotions that are building at the same time. Like a master musician playing me at the perfect tempo, all resistance is given over to the submission of orgasm.

Wiping his mouth before kissing me, I can still taste myself on his tongue. He reaches down to the floor and picks up the condoms. Every time he accidentally or deliberately brushes my body with his, sends a jerking almost embarrassing shock wave though me. He places the tip of his cock, just between my lips. I know it is going to be tight and he'll have to push hard past my tight wet lips. He groans as he penetrates and I know it won't be long for before he climaxes, he is so excited. This doesn't feel like new sex. It doesn't feel like we don't know each other. Being under him, touching his chest and looking into his face as he rides on top of me feels safe, warm and familiar.

He slows his movements: short thrusts then deep ones making his orgasm take longer to build. My pussy is now so tight that as he comes I can feel each pulse and squirt of cum flowing from his cock.

I hate to say it, but I think it might be true when people say, 'She needs to get laid'. I'm not saying that a woman doesn't have a right to mood swings or get really angry without being classed 'hysterical', but lying in Jax's arms, enjoying the post-sex afterglow, I haven't felt so yummy and relaxed in a long time.

Not only has sex put a smile on my face but also my body feels open and totally relaxed now. A weekend of yoga couldn't leave me feeling so satisfied and chilled out. The thing is, I feel vulnerable and a bit shy being that open. Especially after a loud hard orgasm, I get all giggly and childish. I want to push my head into their armpit, stick my tongue in their ear or draw noughts and crosses on the small of their back – any act that might be slightly annoying and break the intimacy of the moment, when it feels like my soul might just open. Not a smart move on a one-night stand, not smart at all! I resist the temptation to see if I can nibble bits off his beard with my teeth and instead ask inane questions about New Year's resolutions.

'To be happy,' he says, 'not get caught up in the bullshit. Travel, go surfing, good times man, just good times. Yours?'

'Bestselling book, sense of belonging somewhere and a growing business.'

'Isn't that goals over resolutions?' He asks.

'OK then, don't screw up.'

'Right, cos we all get to control that!' He laughs.

I roll over to look at the time. I was far away from 'good times', I had an agenda and the clock was ticking. The time is not good and he is reminding me that I might just be missing the point.

I set the alarm, so he won't miss his flight. We fall asleep in each other's arms. I almost never sleep when there's someone close to me. I need my space in bed. But something about the smell of him is really comforting.

It seems like I've just closed my eyes when the alarm goes off. Now this is the worst bit of taking someone home when they are, or you, are drunk. Does he wish you'd turned into a pizza over night? When you open your eyes will you wonder what you were doing as he picks up the skateboard and glides off into the sunrise? I flick off the alarm, turn back to him to find his lips kissing me before pulling me towards him all over again.

He is clear about getting the flight. As he gets out of the bed, he moves the duvet off him bit by bit so no cold air touches my body. It is the sweetest thing. I ask him if he wants the light on, but he says no, it would hurt my eyes and stop me getting back to sleep. He finds his clothes by feeling his way around the room. I ask him to pass me a piece of paper and a pen from the desk, and now I *have* to turn the light on. I write down my number. Taking his phone, he plugs in the number and my phone pings – he's sent me a text so I'll have his number. I know I *know* this might sound like lack of self-esteem, but from what I understand about men, they like to be able to disappear. A man that gives you *his* number likes you. He takes a double look as he walks out of the door. Sitting up in bed, the room feels really big and kind of empty now.

I've made an agreement with myself not to agonise for the next two weeks, just wait to see if I get the chance of a follow-up. I'm not stupid, I am not Demi Moore we are not going to be keeper fish for each other. We will throw each other back into the giant pond of life at some point. I don't quite know how he's got to me like this, but I don't want that to have been it. I would like to swim a while with him.

I'd never had a one-night stand before coming to the USA. That's not to say that I haven't had sex on a first date before, it's just that I have never been someone's one-night stand, as they've always wanted to see me again. I am hoping Jax will be the same. The problem is that I'm still a little bruised about a guy I met at my graduation cohort celebration. Not many of my class managed to get out that night and we ended up in a comedy club. Everyone was peeling off and going home as most of them needed to catch the last BART or bus home. So I sat at the bar and talked to the bartender. He was into British comedy and we started talking about the differences between American and British comedians. We both agreed that Bill Hicks should have been exported more as he was far more British than American humour. He also preferred the British version of *The Office*. All of these bits of conversations were fragmented in-between him serving drinks and trying out his new cocktail concoctions on me.

'What did you think of *Seinfeld*?'

'Loved it. Did you ever see *Spaced*?'

'Only on DVD, it didn't really make it over here.'

'They were going to do a US version of it, like *The Office*.'

'Would never work, *The Office* sucked, you British have smartass humour, we have stupid people humour,' he quipped.

'Only you can say that! What about *Dr Who* and *Sherlock*?'

'Love those shows, *House*?'

'Yes liked *House*, the lead is a Brit.'

'Really?'

'Ever seen *Black Adder*?'

'No.'

'You would never in a million years think it was the same actor, Hugh Laurie, genius!'

'You can bring me that on DVD when you visit home, I have a multi-regional player,' he said giving me the impression there was some kind of future happening evolving.

I didn't realise how drunk I was, until I slid off the bar stool and went to the bathroom. I then knew it was time to do a Cinderella, which is when I realise that I am too drunk for the current situation and need to go home. I then leave, often without saying goodbye to anyone. In this case, I went back to the bar to get my jacket and the chatty bartender asked for my number. He was cute and had got more attractive with every free cocktail that he'd given me to try and I liked talking about my culture's humour.

I thought it would be great to go on a date with him. I hadn't met anyone for the whole year that I'd been in San Francisco, and it seemed perfect to meet someone now I that I had graduated. I hadn't decided if I wanted to stay in the US yet but knew that if I met someone, fell in love and got married then I'd definitely be up for making a permanent home here. To be honest, I want an excuse to stay, rather than my visa running out giving me no choice but to leave. Anyway, quite apart from the cocktails, it was nice to meet someone who liked me and paid me attention. I didn't, however, expect him to call me at 4 a.m. when he finished work.

Like an idiot I woke up and answered the phone and somehow said yes to him coming over. When he arrived I asked him if he wanted a coffee and then stupidly tried to make him one. Of course, he said yes to a coffee, but didn't want one and just started pulling my clothes off in the kitchen. The kitchen backs onto Anna's room and I was worried she would hear us, as she is often up and getting ready for the gym around 6 a.m., so I hurried him off to the bedroom. Which, thinking about it, must have looked like over-enthusiasm for sex, which at that stage I still hadn't fully signed up to having. But it seemed like everything I was doing was very far from protesting that I'd like to get to know him better.

Sex happened quickly and I still hadn't made my mind up by the time it was done and dusted. Afterwards I lay in bed, listening to him breathe with no connection at all and wondering what it had all been about. There is no place in the world that's lonelier than being in your own bed with a disconnected body. I longed to be back in London where at least I'd had my own home. I could have got out of bed and slept on the sofa. In a shared flat you can't do that. I wondered if my desire to meet someone had dissolved my capacity to say 'no' and I'd become desperate or whether my hangover was kicking in and stopping my brain from functioning fully. I felt dry in every way!

Day broke and he left. I was a bit baffled, I don't know what I had been expecting, but I was disappointed. I gave him my number, he didn't leave me his, but I didn't hear from him again. His name was Dean and that's all I know about him apart from where he works.

I know people, I work with people and I am somewhat *bored* with people. I guess what I am looking for is something extraordinary. I have pushed myself to look for the extraordinary too, to be extraordinary perhaps in many areas of life. I've travelled to other cultures, made friends and had lovers who were drugs addicts or users and of various religious views; hobnobbed with celebrities and people who have lived amazing lives, but never dated someone who was *that* much younger than me. Talking to Jax last night, I felt like a kind of vampire who has lived too long, knew too much. When did 'my time' pass me by? I have had to adapt my mind to things we live by now – the Internet, mobile phones and the overload of information that is available now.

Jax was born into that world. Perhaps he is my entry ticket to reconnecting to a time when everything felt possible and there was no such thing as disappointment. I want to taste the ideas he has as they fall from his tongue. I want to feel reconnected to a part of myself. I want to feel confused and vulnerable. I want to be out of my depth. I think he might be the key to these things for me.

I have spent so long working for and with other people for their growth. Part of the feeling of emptiness when I was living back in London was that my life had become ordinary. Busy with no sense of relief, I didn't have time to be at peace with myself to know what that relief was. I used to spend so much time in my head that I was removed from my body. As much as the silence in my life feels empty now, I am the fullest I have been for years.

Thursday 6th January, 2011

Nat pours me a second glass of wine. It has taken the whole of the first glass of wine to give her an almost blow-by-blow account of taking Jax home.

'Oh, my gawd,' she said in her New York accent, 'the dog can wait!'

Now my mother always taught me pets come first, but in this situation that sounds so wrong.

Nat lives in Potrero Hill with an amazing view over the city. From her window you can see one of the main freeways coming into the city and it always seems to have slow-moving traffic no matter what the time of day. I love sitting on her deck, looking out over the lights. Like many San Francisco flats her place is small. It backs onto another flat, half of which is on stilts. This precarious extension seems almost to have been built as an afterthought in a bid to bring in some rental money. Sitting on the stilted deck and looking down the hill of Nat's oddly fused home is the only time that I worry about earthquakes. I drink my wine a little quicker and always get more sloshed at her place.

Her bedroom is the living room, although you would never know because the sofa unfolds to become a bed, and she has an office with a glass wall overlooking the city. The whole flat feels overcrowded with stuff because like so many people who live in San Francisco, New York, Hong Kong, or anywhere where space is at a premium, she has tried to fit forty-four years of life into two rooms. In fact, even the bathroom has a bookshelf!

One entire wall of the office is covered in sticky notes on which Nat's written affirmations, such as 'I love and accept myself completely' or 'I live my life in abundance'. Of course, anyone looking at these notes immediately knows the opposite has to be true because if you lived in abundance, loving and accepting yourself then you wouldn't need to write an affirmation about it. Rather than being happy and not being fussed about what you don't have, you have a written reminder of what you're aiming for and therefore a reminder of what you're missing. I'm pretty sure that focusing on what's missing can only ever lead to feeling unhappy about it and think says something rather poignant about Nat's levels of happiness to anyone visiting her place. Nat doesn't agree and says it's all about goal setting and manifestation.

Nat is an accountant and a business coach. Although she wants to drop the accountancy because the rules and laws keep changing, so she has to keep going through loads of expensive exams to keep up. She loves the business coaching and is really good at it but, with rents in San Francisco being what they are, she needs more clients before she can give up cooking the books.

I met Nat at a singles speed-dating event in a room full of men that might you might expect to meet at the funeral of one of your grandparents, which left us both wondering if we were in the wrong room. Still we sat there waiting politely at our tables, waiting for our dates. When the first guy sat down opposite to me I asked what he did for a living, which was a dumb question as quite clearly he was retired. He was wearing a cravat, like Freddy in Scooby Doo, and said something like, 'I won't talk about work, work is dull and boring, I'm a tango dancer, blah la blah "tango" blah la blah "tango"…'

It was like listening to someone speaking in a foreign language and then every so often the other person comes out with a word in English and it makes you jump as you had zoned out. He was clearly gay not because of the tango, which makes me think of sexy Argentinian men, not even the cravat, but the whole vibe from him was feminine.

'So, what about you?' He finally asked me.

'I'm a workaholic,' I said.

We sat in silence, praying for the one minute and thirty seconds to move faster. On the buzzer to switch tables, he pirouetted round the chair and with a strong leading right leg moved towards Nat's table. She, with a perfect tango stance, stood and as though she had a rose in her teeth strode to my table and said, 'You're British right?'

I nodded mutely.

'Good, we're leaving,' she said and, with that put one hand on my back, took my other hand in hers and tangoed my bubbling polite British ass out of the door and so, with just one final back bend to check that I hadn't forgotten anything at the table, we left.

From that moment, I fell in love with her. I admired her powerful dynamism from the get-go. She gave me no choice about staying at that table. I had to join her and that first meeting really sums up our friendship ever since. I am the friendless one in a new town, so am always at the mercy of what she wants to do because I don't know what I am doing and she does.

Nat is also single and believes she manifested me because she wanted a single girlfriend to go out looking for guys with. She is teaching me the ways of American dating, or rather San Francisco dating as that seems to be a whole different world. Lots of gay men come to San Francisco to live in a place where being gay is openly accepted and sometimes a requirement. So the straight men are living in a chocolate box filled to overflowing with other gay men and women who ALL want the rareness of that commodity, a straight cock. They really know how to play it too, and many of them are the Peter Pan of non-attachment. Why should they? There are enough soft centres to choose from in the sexual assortment box!

Nat won't date any of the bridge-and-tunnel crowd (meaning anyone who doesn't live in the forty-seven or so square miles of San Francisco). That's not a wide area and that's not a lot of men but she is clear on her rule. I believe in limits of potential, Nat believes you'll manifest your negative beliefs. She has walked away from many an OK relationship because she longs for that sense of desire that I believe you only get from NOT being with the person you love.

Now Nat's perpetual sense of desire seems to be turning into morbid dissatisfaction. She believes it is completely possible to have it all in one man: the excitement, the desire and the security, love warmth and companionship. I don't but then Nat thinks I have negative belief patterns and so won't 'manifest' the perfect man. She is holding out for all of those things to come in one package. I really hope she finds it.

My mum has a saying: 'You need two men. One to bring up the kids with and one for great sex, and it's not possible to find them both in the same man.'

I was shocked when she said it, but listening to my clients I think she might be right.

Tonight Nat and I are staying in but we love to cross Golden Gate Bridge to Cavallo Point for a glass of wine. Marin is really beautiful and the people there are wealthy, I think Nat might make an exception and date a guy from there. We always sit at the bar, as you're more likely to get chatted up than sitting at a table – another dating strategy I've learnt from Nat.

Last time we were there, I got talking to the bartender who was really nice. Not amazing looking but as he talked he became more and more attractive. He told me that he'd taken a bar job because he was burnt out from working with abused children. I told Nat I liked him and she exclaimed she does too, and before I knew it she was putting her card under her empty glass and telling me, 'You need to move fast in this town,' which made me gasp.

The barman looked at her card then at me, saw her photo and shot me an odd glance, before thanking her.

It was soon after that happened that I started calling myself her handbag caddy. I've found that whenever we go out dancing, some guy will cut across me to dance in front of Nat. Like I'm not even there! Then we end up doing some kind of country-dance do-si-do as I dance back around him to dance in front of her again. Then he will dance round me again. So the next time I do-si-do I use my elbows, like I am doing the *Birdy Dance*. I have no problem with people wanting to dance with her. I get it! She's tall, thin, blonde and blue eyed – but can't they dance with both of us? Why cut in front of me? Every time we stand at the bar at singles nights, Nat is asked to dance and gives me her handbag to hold. Leaving me on my own, holding a drink and two handbags. Needless to say I never get asked to dance.

Being a Brit living in the States, I find I can't navigate the boy-meet-girl scene here. I flirt by being funny but the Americans take my jokes seriously. Nat gets my jokes and often steps in to interpret them for me, telling the bemused guy, 'She's jok*ing*.'

Nat has an interesting face but she has a wide mouth that seems too heavy for her face so it turns downwards and makes her look sad. When we first met I was always asking her if she was 'Alright?' This was partly due to my own insecurity because she often looked pissed off after I'd asked. I've finally got it that she just has one of those faces. Making her laugh is kind of addictive because whenever she smiles it is SO big that her whole face lights up with it. She is like one of those double-sided Greek theatre masks – comedic one side, tragic the other. Making her happy fills me with confidence too. So it's a win-win.

I worry that I've become a bit impish and have lost the art of sexual communication. In fact, sometimes I wonder whether I've lost the art of communication itself. I have become socially awkward and my misunderstood sense of humour seems to portray me as being a bit of a sociopath. The problem is I can't conform to social norms that I simply don't understand, and only know that I've crossed the line when I'm greeted with the blank and, sometimes shocked, face of some unsuspecting male.

Psychological studies have scientifically proven that if you don't fit in, you don't do well. The University of Minnesota ran some tests with college students and those students who had a sense of belonging to the university did better in test scores than those who felt like they didn't fit in. Over a number of years, the study noted that those students from multicultural backgrounds who were made to feel welcome did as well as their white counterparts; but those for whom no effort was made did worse in test scores. Try walking into a biker bar wearing a suit and joining a game of darts, no way in hell will you hit the board. Go in sporting a leather jacket and you'll do fine, even if you leave the bar for the car park and ride off on a Vespa!

Nat doesn't have much confidence in my New Year Eve's sex-caspades she thinks the age gap means that Jax is a waste of time. She says, 'Just enjoy it for what it was, sweetie, it's not like you'll be seeing *him* again. 'Before adding, 'If I were you, I wouldn't give it another thought.'

Nat has also just met someone who's she's hoping will call but hasn't yet. He lives in Knob Hill and told her which block he lives on, so we decide to do a drive-by. Knob Hill is one of the most expensive areas to live in San Francisco, so I guess she wants to see *how* expensive! Nat drives a stick shift, which is tough with all the hills but I enjoy driving around the city, especially at night. It's very beautiful when all the buildings are lit up.

When we get to the right block, Nat laughs and says he's so far on the edge of Knob Hill he's in the Tenderloin – also known as the 'Tender Knob' in the city's zip code, house price and rental market war. The Tenderloin district is rough and I wouldn't want to go there at night. Most of the places for rent are just one-room-with-shared-bathroom dives, so people sit out on the street and watch TV because it's better than being indoors. It's odd that it is right next door to one of the most prestigious neighbourhoods in San Francisco, which has some of the highest rents. Rich and the poor divided by the size of a hill.

Nat dropped the dog and me home after our reconnaissance mission. Later in bed, I start thinking about my life back home. In London I had become a workaholic and lost a sense of who I was – an empty vessel living on wine and takeaways. I came to San Francisco to be a student but also to relaunch my life in what I thought was a spiritual utopia – California. Mostly I believe I was expecting to fall madly in love with an American dream guy and move to a beautiful house by the beach, where I'd write fantastic self-help books for other people, who were as bad as I was at helping themselves.

I started Internet and speed dating as soon as I arrived in the States. After all, I had a cute British accent, had just lost weight and was feeling optimistic. Then the clanger –having a book on relationships published while being single. It just doesn't look good to have an online dating profile on match.com when you're supposed to be a relationships expert.

I think writing the book has *made* me single. I know exactly what I want from a man: I have researched it, lived it and breathed it. I became all consumed by love while I was writing the book, it's hiding in plain sight but I just can't see what I'm missing for overlooking it. It's OK, I've accepted not falling in love and going back to the UK at the end of this year to start again – yet again. Right now, I am in the moment of ultimate potential: I am not where I was, not where I am going, I'm in the now. The anxiety is often raw and sometimes invigorating.

Saturday 15th January

There might just be a romantic in everyone. After the excitement of meeting Jax on New Year's Eve and the obvious ego boost it's given me, I've decided to make full use of the Mojo and get back into dating as Nat suggested. I don't have long left before my visa expires to mess around waiting for a guy that I know I have no future with, so have been on a few dates in the past week.

Last Monday I went on a date with a guy called Rick, who seemed to have almost lived the same life as me: travelled, owned motorbikes, raced cars, done dangerous sports. I think he was pretty excited to finally meet a woman who understood his life choices. He also told me that he has entered into the more kinky side of sexual relations. I was intrigued and he took great delight in telling me about the various sex clubs in San Francisco. He seemed to love the fact that I asked him questions and wasn't shocked. I could almost hear him thinking: *Here at last is a woman who understands me.*

Sadly, I could feel more sexually attracted to a toilet brush; it must be the spiky bristles! It's hardly ever about a man's looks for me, more the vibe of the person, a look in their eyes even. I got nothing of that from him and, in fact, the more I sat talking to him, the more drained I started to feel.

At one point during the evening, he pointed at some

of the other diners in the restaurant and made a comment about why we (he and I) were better than all of the people sat around us and said, 'Look at those people they've never travelled or done anything interesting.'

He then went on to talk about his school friends on Facebook who he mocked for having raised kids and adventure-less lives. His mass generalisations and self-congratulation irritated me and when I offered up an opinion or objection, he just talked over me. So I stopped saying anything and just listened, feeling withdrawn and lonely.

But towards the end of the meal, I saw my chance to speak. By that point I knew if things went down badly I could leave because the meal was over. I hate to see good food going to waste but when I'm in conflict, my throat closes and I can't eat – and I was determined to get something good out of the evening. So I held back from telling him that he was coming across like an arrogant knob head right until the last mouthful. OK so I didn't call him a 'knob head', instead I decided to tell him who he was being by using the art form of self-reflected story as metaphor. So I leaned across the table and, as he leaned back towards me and held my gaze, I started to open up to him and told him something deeply personal to me.

'When I lived in London,' I said, 'I had a wall of photos in my house lit with spotlights running down the stairs to the basement bedrooms.'

'I love basement bedrooms,' He interjected with a kind of *ooh good dungeon* insinuation.

'Shut up, I'm talking now!'

He looked a bit shocked at being told to shut up and likely put it down to cultural discrepancy. It wasn't, I was being rude and meant it. Then a glint came into his eyes and I realised he was back in the dungeon. I knew at least that I had his attention so I carried on.

'It was like an art gallery of all the great places I have been. All the iconic tourist shots and some arty ones, most of which starred my grinning face. It was guaranteed that people would see them as they made their way downstairs to the bathroom. In fact you couldn't see down the stairs unless the lights, which highlighted my pride and joy, were turned on.

'I took those photos and made that gallery so that people would think I was an amazingly well-travelled person: cultural, interesting and with real things to say about the world from experience. The sad thing is, the more you do and see the less people are interested in your stories. People only want to hear stories they can relate to, or say something that can bond the connection between the listener and the teller.

'I did all this travelling, hung out with cool people, collected and appropriated objects from around the world because I felt so empty inside. I had to build a very big definition of who I was by where I'd been and what I'd done. In life you are stuck because you're scared or you're running because you're scared. You and I have everything in common with the people here sitting around us...It's fear. You think love is the driving force behind your life; it's not, it's fear. We just tell ourselves stories to make our lives better. It's good to tell yourself a positive story about yourself. But you can't sit here and drop other peoples' values to make your valued greater.'

That stream of consciousness felt better. Check please!

Rick looked at me with a sympathetic eye but didn't understand a word of it.

Deep down, I knew that everything that had irritated me about him all evening was everything that I am guilty of too, and was possibly the reason why I ran away from my wall of interesting life experiences and am now trying to create a new one by being a foreigner. I always find myself more interesting when I am the outsider.

'But all of that experience,' he said, 'does make you better than everyone else in this room. Most people here have done half the things you have and are boring because of it.'

'You're not hearing me,' I told him. 'It makes me less interesting. People stay still because they are too scared to move and people move because they are too scared to stay still. Fear is the matching motivation. I am no different from any other person in this room, we all just reacting to a different definition of fear. All fear is the same. It feels the same; it's just how we react to it that is different.

'Living without fear is the key. I now finally don't care what people think of me, or who I am. I only care about tuning into the real authentic me so that I can grow as a person. Anything I have to show or prove to other people will only exclude me from them. The travelling and crazy lifestyle was due to being insecure. I thought it would make me secure and it did in a hardened-survivor kind of way. I have only ever been fighting me. Not circumstances or my luck, just my own perception of who I am. Anyone else's perception of me is inaccurate and yet I have spent my life listening to other peoples' opinions of me in order to meet and learn who I am. So if someone thought I was amazing it made me amazing. But then when you're on your own, and the lights are out in a dark room, who are you then? Who *are* you then!'

After this outburst, I think he saw me as some kind of wounded lamb who would be a dominatrix if only she could find her magic PVC slippers. He didn't see me as the best place I could possibly be: comfortable in chaos and insecurity. Not hiding it, having it out there in the world as a real part of who I am. So I did what any self-respecting fully empowered woman would do. I left him some cash to pay the bill and went home and, with a few glasses of wine under my belt as an excuse, texted Jax. I know, I know, my number one rule broken – don't chase the boy! Keep it light and airy.

> Hope u r enjoying Seattle, call me up when you get back if you would like some more fireworks.

Two minutes later – *beep!*

> Hey, had a great time tonight! When's our second date? Rick x

Oh, *bugger bollocks*! I had thought I'd made myself clear in the restaurant when I'd stalked out without a backward glance.

Dating is complex. I knew I shouldn't have gone out on a first date with him as he reminded me of an ex-boyfriend Brian who was a bit of an obsessive control freak and the events of that first date with Rick proved me right. But against my better intuition I talked myself into it. As it turned out, he *was* just like my ex-boyfriend. Perhaps ex-boyfriend is overstating the relationship, we were only together three months. Brian had this idea that he had to do everything 'to the max', as he put it. He just didn't have an off switch.

People who are that intense in their energy often don't have a balance point. So they can't hear you fully. Whatever you say becomes about them, it's a sort of narcissism and so they are very difficult to have a conversation with. Although it can be good in one way because that type usually wants to fix all your problems. The only thing is they often fix them with a little bit too much force, and our relationship came to abrupt end when my goldfish got sick.

I had decided to set it free in a large pond so it could be free from the tank it had overgrown and because I think it was bored senseless being the only fish left. Although I have a sneaking suspicion that it may have killed the other two. Anyway, knowing it wouldn't live much longer we took it to a lake in the local park. I planned to put the bag in the water and let the water get to the right temperature before letting the fish free slowly in a kind of ritual and meaningful goodbye. I love fish but this was to be my last fish. I never again wanted to take an animal and put it in an un-natural environment.

When we got to the lake, Brian took the bag from me and ripped it open with his fingers, so the fish fell onto the bank. Then he picked it up and chucked it into the water. I was devastated. I believe there are some things that happen in a relationship that a woman will never let go of. It's like a picture in her mind that she plays time and time again. Often during sex, she will see the image or the emotions of the act. She may never express it, but sex will never feel right again. Her legs will be open, but her soul will be closed. Unless the man can reopen her, the relationship will die. He may never know why; she may never be able to tell him. That goldfish moment was one of those moments.

Monday 17th January

So, after dickhead-three-month fling (can't really call it a relationship) clone, I've just got back from date number two in the same week; this time with a guy called Robert – look at me go! Although the evening didn't get off to a great start because I barely recognised him when he arrived. He didn't look anything like his dating profile, more like he had just stepped out of the Shire in *The Hobbit,* with spiky reddish hair and arms and legs that looked too long for his body. We had arranged to go to dinner in an Indian restaurant, one he proudly told me that Obama had eaten in. You can't really say 'no' to eating in the same place as the president of the United States of America. Not that we were going to be eating with Obama. Sitting opposite each other, I asked him what he planned to drink, thinking we could get a bottle of wine. But before I'd finished the sentence, I realised he didn't drink. So I asked him if he'd mind if I have a beer.

He said, 'No, go right ahead if you want to kill yourself like that.'

I laughed, but he wasn't joking. When the beer came it had the sexiest beer glass I think I have ever seen, with the curves of a woman and so cold that it looked like it had frost all over it. I poured it slowly, loving the look of the amber liquid filling the very cold glass. He asked me to wait as he took my glass of beer placed his hands around it and started to pray. This would have been reasonably amusing but his lips moving in murmur went on and on, and my glass of beer got warmer and warmer. When he finished, he handed me back the beer saying, 'It's safe to drink now, I have taken all of the poisons out of it.'

I would have laughed and thought him mad, however, there was an element of Harry Potter's best mate about him and I started to worry his magical powers had removed the alcohol content. He laughed and told me that he can make cheap bottles of wine taste expensive by using healing to take out all the impurities, and that his friends love inviting him to parties. That was the highlight of our date and the rest of the evening was like having dinner with occultist Aleister Crowley.

Nat met up with me after my date – we'd arranged to meet up after I'd sent her a text from the bathroom asking to be rescued from the Hobbit. When I told her about the evening she said, 'Why is dating this difficult, it should be a matter of boy meets girl, jiggy jiggy!'

I couldn't help but think of Jax.

The guy Nat has been seeing is away on business and she's concerned by the lack of texting. One day she hears from him and the next day she doesn't. I gave her a PDF copy of my book and said she should read the section on 'how to control anxiety in new dating'. As I did so, I mentally reread what I'd written and realised that what I have to say is really good, and I should try it some time!

I have inspired Nat to write a book too, so she's doing a course on how to write a book in a weekend. I can't believe that a book written in a weekend could possibly be any good. Things that are difficult feel of more value when they are done. In the same way that a packet muffin mix is not the same as a muffin you make yourself from scratch. It's called the 'Ikea effect', which is when you value something more because you put time and effort into making or building it. I wonder if this is why relationships last longer when they start with a story. The kind of thing you tell your grandchildren about, which becomes embellished over time. It might also explain why guys tend stay longer in a relationship and have fewer affairs if they had to chase their partner. Just coming out with some scientific facts about human nature! Perhaps it's why it often goes against a woman if she sleeps with a guy on the first meeting, or even second meeting.

The problem Nat and I discussed this evening is that we are in touch with our masculine sides. We chase men! Men are the chasers and women are the choosers. However, in San Francisco the men are emotionally fat and unfit because the deer are plentiful and desperate. Why should they bother drawing an arrow when there's a plethora of females happy to simply fall to the ground on their backs with their legs open grunting, snorting and bleating? Making deer noises nearly made us fall off our bar stools laughing, particularly because we don't even know what noise a deer makes.

We got some filthy looks from the guys for laughing during the ball game – that'll teach Nat and I for choosing a sports bar as a compromise between her love of dives and my love of wine bars. However, after my disastrous date and Nat's lack of texting action, we enjoyed sucking up the male testosterone. Sports bars are not for me, Nat loved it, but I guess I know more about the ball game now than the cool adverts in-between them!

Tuesday 18th January

I wish I could pull the book back from the publishers and add some of my recent dating stories. Self-help books about relationships are always written from the viewpoint of compatibility. Not very helpful when there's a lack of similar fish or rather the ocean is full of sharks, or guppies.

The book is coming out soon and I have to get over feeling like an idiot for being single. I have been spending my days sending out press releases, making calls and trying to drum up interest. I have a few interviews lined up, one with a radio station in Seattle, where Jax is now. But we haven't got a date in the diary yet. I think I might go to Seattle rather than do the interview over the phone. I'd love to visit the Space Needle and see all the places that were on *Grey's Anatomy* – even if it isn't actually filmed there.

Of course, there's a bit of me that's kind of hoping that I will be going with Jax. I know how ridiculous I am being, but he's got into my head and now thoughts of him seem to be polluting everything. If I go shopping and try on clothes, I wonder if he would like what I am wearing. I am irritating myself, I know I am the thinker of my thoughts and I can turn them off. The problem is I am enjoying them. I can feel the rush of oxytocin-laced excitement and the sensation of my jeans rubbing against my crotch as my thoughts take a sexual turn. I'm sure if I were really busy with clients and a bestselling book, Jax wouldn't feature so prominently in my mind. But what can I say, it is what it is and sometimes the fantasy is much better that the reality.

Wednesday 19th January

Jax is due back any day now, I think. Still no text but plenty from Rick the motorbike, ex-boyfriend clone. He even sent me a text earlier today saying:

> I can feel your pain and I know how to heal you.☺

Oh, cock off! Every time I get a text I hope it is Jax, which makes me even more annoyed than I would be otherwise. The bloody smiley face that he keeps texting me, just so I won't forget him, is infuriating. But unless Jax writes back now that he's home, I am going to have to get some personal discipline and give up the ghost on that one.

I had to go to a café today to help my boss do some training on how they can make their café more environmentally friendly. I usually work from home and mostly social media stuff for the coffee shops that are members of Green Café. Tweeting their Tweets, finding coffee shops to follow and posting information on our Facebook page. However, the business owner, a one-woman-band called Carol, thought it would be a good idea if I could Tweet and write a blog about her coffee shop's experience of getting its Californian green certification.

I wished I could remember the name of the place

where Jax works, not to become a stalker but so I can avoid looking like a stalker! I would just love to see him one last time. For a man I hardly know, I know I'm being ridiculous. I am just frightened that this is going to start adding up to a pattern of letdowns. So, I just want the taste of intrigue to last longer than one night and twenty-one days of thinking about it. I don't want to make this mean that my move to the US was the wrong one. It's so easy to make things mean things that they don't mean.

I have to be honest I don't understand the dating culture here. This is partly due to the fact that my best chat-up lines rely on my sense of humour, which seems totally lost on most of the men I meet. Take, for example, this guy Bruce that I met on an online dating site. He was very muscular, which I am not normally into. He was also very into himself and told me he was 'sex positive'. I thought this had something to do with being HIV so I spent a good part of our conversation thinking how brave he was to tell me about it on our first date – and also that it was tantamount to emotional blackmail! Now if I didn't like him, he'd think it was because he was HIV and I would feel bad.

However, it turned out that being sex positive is a Californian thing about being really open and non-judgemental about sexuality. I am still not quite sure I fully understand what he was talking about but, from the sound of it, it's got something to do with having multiple partners – a bit like polygamy but without any of the commitment. I sent a text to Nat while he was in the toilet and asked her what sex positive meant. She wrote back one word:

Slut.

He also called himself a 'burner', which is someone who goes to the Burning Man Festival every year. This seems to be some kind of religious way of life and it's a great place to have an epiphany apparently. I can't even imagine what this is like because all I can see is Glastonbury Festival, but set in the desert. Bruce worked very hard to identify who he was to me but, without any of the reference points, him being called a 'burner' didn't really make any sense to me. Of course, if he'd have said he was an 'Olympic athlete', I would have known what that was; or a 'Mormon', I would have got that too. But he said 'burner' with such conviction that I just felt embarrassed, almost as if I'd failed to recognise Michael Jackson at a disco.

He didn't get me either and my few jokes either went over his head or he took them in earnest. The best moment came when I went to the bathroom for the second time. I hate making people wait, so I took a pee, washed my hands and came right back to him without reapplying my make-up, messing about or texting Nat with an update.

'That was quick,' he said.

'Didn't wash my hands,' I quipped back.

'Oh my God, that is so HOT!'

Shit! Do I tell him I am joking or do I just keep smiling?

'That is so hot! You wanted to get back to me so fast that you didn't wash your hands,' he said again in wonderment.

There is no way I can tell him now that I am joking and I did wash my hands. He then goes on to tell me that he is OCD about hand washing and wouldn't even open the door in a bar bathroom without using a hand towel. Now I really can't tell him I am joking.

At the end of the evening, he kissed me at my front door, which was obviously part of his being sex positive and his way of telling me that he wouldn't judge me if I shagged him on our first date. I had a good feel of his body through his clothes and on paper I should have been creaming my pants – on loo paper that is, tee hee! The problem was, he knew it. You know those people who look at their own reflection in windows? Well he was one of those. I could see him riding on top of me while kissing his own arms and asking, 'You like these guns, baby?'

I told him I had to walk the dog, and he said he would like to come too, so not heading towards the bushes of Dolores Park that's for sure, as I am sure he would also be very sex positive about doing it in public too!

Now I have an exceptional dog. OK I am sure all dog mums and dads feel like this, but my dog taught herself to step off the pavement to do her business. So when she nipped onto the road to take a crap, I was so proud that I forgot all about his OCD and proudly pointed it out to him. His face was a picture when I had to pick up the dog poo in a bag. Strangely, he didn't call me again and the offer of a shag fell off the loo seat.

Thursday 20th January

Success! I got a text from Jax. We have a date for tomorrow night at the 500 Club where we first met. I have decided to decide that I am not nervous but, in fact, excited – as the two emotions feel more or less the same. I'm also relieved that he has got in touch as I'm sure hanging with my sulky face wouldn't be fun much longer if he hadn't.

The day we're meeting up is the Mission Dive Bar Meet Up Group. The idea of these get-togethers is that you pick a dive bar, contact the owner and make a deal with them along the lines of, 'I can bring a large group of people to your bar for one night, if you give everyone with a name badge a deal on alcohol'. So that might be a discount on the price of the drink or two-for-one happy hour all night. Now dive bars are often pretty rough and most people wouldn't want to go in there on their own but once a month, on this sacred night, the bar gets packed with a mob of drinking buddies who like dive bars and spend the night swilling back cheap booze.

As you'd imagine, it attracts women like bees to a honeypot, but oddly many of them are Asians and, when it comes to picking up guys, they usually beat the average white girl hands down. Nat really loves going, well I've already said, she has a thing for dive bars. Me, I often find it hard to talk to the people who go to this meet-up.

Not because they are drunk but because I am terrible at small talk. Again, the more I drink the funnier I think I'm being and the less funny people think I am, and so I end up drinking more to make up for not being funny.

The original idea of Nat and I going to this meet-up was to meet guys. You know what though? Guys that hang out in dive bars are likely to be dive-bar guys, and I guess I see myself with a man who is a professional. Someone with a passion and knows one end of a bottle of wine from the other. I guess I would like to meet a wine-bar guy.

Nat and I have discussed this, but one of the problems with California is that everyone is very healthy and not that many people seem to drink. At least the dive-bar guys don't think I'm an alcoholic – probably because they *are* alcoholics. Drinking is part of the British culture, which probably has something to do with having to maintain a stiff upper lip and being repressed – the booze helps us find freedom of expression. Nat enjoys drinking but our joint exploits in online dating have thrown up far too many Californian men who enjoy hiking, outdoor pursuits, surfing, a day of bike riding, snowboarding, vegetarianism and so on. All of which turns her on like a sack of potatoes. At least the dive-bar men are not into hiking. For starters, most of them can't see their feet on a flat surface but then Nat's not really into beer bellies either. She still believes she will get what she wants in a man, and may be she will with the Knob Hill guy. Somewhere there has to be a compromise.

I feel a little bit awkward about meeting Jax among these people. But I don't want to wait somewhere for him on my own. Frankly, I don't expect us to stay long – but it does mean the bar will be packed.

A terrifying thought has just crept over me...*I bloody hope I can remember what he looks like!*

Saturday 22nd January

Last night was the Mission Dive Bar Meet Up, and as I predicted waiting for Jax in the crowded bar was really uncomfortable. I was like a meerkat watching the door: jumping up and looking around, small talking with a bozo and looking back at the door. I also managed to get into an argument with a guy who thought I was really an American and putting on a British accent. He told me that he is part Irish and supports the IRA. He knew absolutely nothing about the conflict, although he thought he did and decided to insult the British as a way to get me to admit that I was, in fact, an American. Nat genially requested that I didn't whip the floor with his brain cells. It was too late, I extracted the one brain cell he had been using to fire facts about Ireland, inspected it under my fingernail before stepping in for the kill.

You see, I spent five years of my childhood living in Dingle, the furthest west point of Ireland, and my mother is as Irish as they come. So I mixed this information with some US politics through one of his ears and the rest of his brain cells oozed out of the other. I think I might have kicked a few of them on the way to the bathroom to calm down. When I came back, he'd gone.

I've noticed how I keep making these sorts of social mistakes. Once when I was at a dinner party with someone from my college course, another guest asked me what I thought of American politics, so I told her. At the time we were drinking wine out of jam jars and had mismatching plates, knives and forks and everyone was talking about how right on it was to save the environment, so I thought I was with some really radical people. In retrospect, I realise that Russell Brand and I might have a lot in common because, while I didn't call Bush a retard, I knew I must have gone wrong somewhere along the line when the host clapped her hands and said, 'Puppies and kittens, puppies and kittens everyone.'

Everyone replied, 'Puppies and kittens.'

I asked later what it was about and was told I was being too negative and should never talk politics even when someone asks you, it's vulgar!

Jax was late and, although I knew he'd come, the tennis looks towards the door were starting to give me whiplash. Then I noticed a guy I had gone on a few dates with, kept walking past me in a drive-by kind of way. He was staring at me and acting weird. I was now desperate to get out of there. In the end, I called him. Now I know this is so not the thing to do but by this time, he was a Californian time forty-five minutes late. I tried to sound really cheery, like I was calling in case I'd missed him because the bar was so packed. I don't know why we do that bullshit to ourselves! Who are we kidding? We might as well say, 'Hey, you're super late, just calling to see if you've stood me up, as I am feeling like a right tit right now.' Luckily I managed to cough up my 'Mrs Free-and-Easy bollocks' and he told me that he was only a few blocks away.

Nat saw him come through the door first and

chucked me one of her blue-eyed *there's your man* looks. We have had many a conversation with our eyes. Mostly it's Nat communicating things like *button it, I fancy him*, or *another drink?* I enjoy non-verbal conversations and Nat and I are very good at telling jokes with our eyes and making social comments, such as when we think someone is being a twat.

I parted the sea of people and almost fell on Jax because somehow my legs weren't working properly, either that or I got my foot stuck on someone else's leg, and the top half of my body moved forward without the bottom half. We started kissing before we had really said a word to each other. I stood at the bar and got us both a beer, but we didn't finish drinking them before we were heading for the door and the privacy of my bedroom.

On the way back to the flat, Jax explained that he was nervous, which is why he was late. That made me feel much better and I was able to say how nervous I was. In fact I was so nervous I was kind of shaking with adrenaline. I think that's kind of why we fell on each other. Kissing was a much more effective icebreaker than talking. He looked even better than I remembered. I think his mom must have been feeding up because he looked kind of rounder, but in a good way. He kept giving gave me these blue-eyed appraisals that started as sideways glances and then moved up and at me though his eyebrows, even though I am shorter than him. Making eye contact didn't see that easy for him so we just kept kissing, which meant he could simply keep them closed. I could feel his heart racing thought his T-shirt and the warmth of his anticipation though the heat of the blood in his lips. I wanted to suck and even bite them just a bit, but it seemed too much so

I just let my tongue move over the top of them in a stolen moment between kisses.

This time, he was naked when I came back into the room from taking the dog out for a pee. He looked so beautiful that I stopped in the doorway and just looked. He walked over to me and put one hand onto the back of my neck and into my hair, while closing the door with the other. We stood there awhile, just kissing and touching, I was still shaking and trying to hide it. When he pulled back to bring me closer to the bed, my face burrowed into the slight hair on his chest and I breathed him in. He made a noise like what I had done was cute. He undid the first two buttons of my blouse and pulled it off over my head. The cool air on my skin was all part of the eroticism of the moment. Tracing his tongue down my neck and allowing the trail of saliva to go cold behind him, my body let out a shiver. He pulled me into his chest, wrapped his arms around me as he undid my trousers and allowed them to fall to the floor. I stepped out of them and my shoes. He spent time rubbing my clitoris through my wet pants. Best pants of course, black lace with a white trim in an old-fashioned style. I felt sexy in them and he clearly liked the texture of my wet pussy beneath. Without removing them, he opened them up to the side and slid his cool fingers into my hot vagina. Rolling the folds around with his fingers, my breath got faster and I longed for the security of the bed under my buckling knees. He pulled me down on top of him, my legs neatly straddling his cock. I rubbed him over my knickers making his erect cock wet. Lifting my bum in the air, I moved down his body into a yoga downward-facing dog pose so I could take his cock into my mouth and remove my knickers with the other hand. Not caring,

I slid them over off one leg and left them dripping from my other foot.

I liked being about to taste myself on him, an amalgamation of both of our arousals all taking place on my lips and tasting exquisitely on my tongue. It made me want to taste more of him, so I sucked him a little harder and as I did so he let out just a drop of pre-cum, which I rolled around his cock with my tongue. Moving up between his legs, I opened him up wide so I could crouch my small body between his strong thighs. I used my hands and ran my fingers up the inside of his legs. He massaged the back of my neck and made approving groans, which just made me want to please him more.

Taking one hand I wrapped it around the base of his penis and gripped tightly, forcing the blood to gather at the end of his cock, making it bulbous and sensitive. I licked, sucked and used my wet lips, so that they felt like a tight vagina, as I let him penetrate my mouth over and over again. I licked my hand and clasping his cock firmly, I pulled slowly down to create a restriction on the way down and then a release on the way up. His groaning and cries of 'Oh God' were intensifying. I loved having this much control over him, so I slowed it right down, to delay his build towards orgasm.

Breathing deeply now he said, 'I really want to fuck you now!'

Muttering 'Not yet,' I moved down to his balls, licking and sucking while continuing the slow and sensitive movements on the end of his cock.

His groans got louder and more desperate; I could feel he was close to begging me, when he let out a small whimper, 'Please.'

So, I took his cock back into my mouth and used my fingers over his balls, pushing in circles against his G-spot. This was now too much and he pulled me back up his body gently but firmly by my hair, grabbed at where the condoms were last time, rolled one on as he pushed me onto my back. My legs fell open and he let out a grunt as he pushed his way in. He arched up on his arms so I could see his chest in the half-light from the window, his pecks standing out tense as his arms took the weight of his torso. My fingers slipped between my crevice to feel his hard cock pumping in and out of me. I started to play with my clit, the response was fast and I could feel my orgasm starting to build as I moved in a circle every time he moved out and my fingers were squashed hard onto my clit every time he pushed in. As my pussy got tighter and wetter, my breathing turned into gasps and cries, I could feel him starting to reach climax but knew I wasn't ready.

Jax must have had the same idea, because he slowed down, which must have been agonising when he was so close. Then it happened, I started to orgasm hard, gripping his neck with my hand and burying my face into his chest to muffle my cries. He stopped to kiss my face and lips, and then to my dismay pulled out. But only for a moment, as he rolled me onto my front and closed my legs, before finding a way to push his cock back into me. He pushed in, held it still for a moment like a composer about to conduct an orchestra and then started fucking me fast and hard. I pushed back against the pillow, the whole of my body held tight and gripping, as he fucked me like an animal, over and over relentlessly.

I know I asked for this by being such a tease, and was thankful that my legs were together as it was hard enough to handle his size. His hand gripped my shoulder and just when I began to think I just couldn't take any more he shot into me. With each spurt, he pushed even deeper, filling me up with nowhere else to go.

'Oh my fucking God,' he said and collapsed next to me. 'Jesus, you're gonna kill me!'

Loving the compliment and thinking with age comes practice, but then with age comes...age! After that, we lay there for a while, just breathing and holding each other. I could feel him drifting in and out of consciousness as he started to fall sleep and wake again. He had no idea he was doing it but I didn't want to lose his company, not just yet. So I asked him the question that was buzzing around my mind. I really wanted to know if he could feel the difference between my body and a girl of his own age.

I know it was a stupid question, but I dated a guy with a large age gap and his skin had felt like rubber. I could pull the skin on his elbow and it would have made a rain hat! So I asked him and immediately wished I hadn't. He paused, a long pause, and I started to hope he had nodded off.

'To be honest,' he said, 'I'm mostly thinking about your pussy.'

Then I felt a little foolish. After all, I should know by now that men don't think the same way as women, 'I'm mostly thinking about your pussy' – classic!

He told me more about his family and his trip home. He's really excited about his new place, which has one room with a bathroom. My blood went cold thinking about the places in the Tenderloin like that, which Nat had told me about. He was so excited to be getting his own place and away from his cousin's nagging girlfriend. Without speaking its name, he described where it was and it is definitely in the Tenderloin. I am sure he can take care of himself but my heart sank. We talked about the skill of making decent coffee in the coffee shop where he works and how they have a bakery attached to the coffee house. He does the deliveries in the morning, which is why he has to get there for 5.30 a.m. for his shift. But he enjoys being done by 3 p.m. He told me he wants to be a film director and/or scriptwriter.

I had made a short film with the students of the drama department where I taught in London at City Lit, an adult education college in Covent Garden. They needed an actress my age and I did it for a bit of fun. It was a zombie movie and I quite enjoyed my tragic demise as my body parts fell off during the filming and I loved the horror make-up – although I'd had to rub so hard to get the blood out of my ears that I got a slight ear infection.

Jax reminded me of a younger version of the man who directed and wrote the screenplay. Jax told me he was trying to write a script about the fictional life of Kurt Cobain's daughter. Jax has the kind of fairy dust that would make a great film director: a unique way of seeing the world, a commentator on the human condition. It kind of made me feel excited to be in his presence. Like discovering a band that you know are going to be really big. I felt the same way when I went to see Radiohead at Glastonbury Festival before they made the big time. Standing close to singer Thom Yorke, I remember needing the bathroom but would have rather wet my knickers on the spot than give up my place on the front row. I don't think I've had such an interesting conversation about nothing much in a long time. I know I am going to change him. I hope it's for the better. I want to give him things that he doesn't even know to ask for, because he has never experienced them.

Later that night Jax had a bad dream. He was moaning and thrashing around and not in a good way! I don't think he was fighting monsters; it seemed more like a panic attack but while he was sleeping. I tried to soothe him by stroking the back of his neck and behind his ears. Then I realised that's what I do with the dog. Rubbing a dog's ears releases endorphins and makes them feel relaxed. Not sure the same thing works on humans, but I didn't know what else to do, fall short of waking him up. But it did work and he started murmuring nicely and was sleeping in no time. Who knew! I get the feeling that he is often full of anxiety and trying really hard to hide it. I told him in the morning, just as he was leaving for work that he'd been talking in his sleep. He brushed it off, so I said, 'You must have been eating too much cheese.'

He looked at me like I had spoken in Dutch, '*What?*'

He had never heard the common theory that cheese can give you weird dreams, and it made me realise how much I didn't know at his age or what is shared from one culture to the next. American films and song lyrics make much more sense to me now that I live here. Stupid pointless bits of information that now I understand in context. I used to love Prince and thought his song *Little Red Corvette* was so sexy. I did a dance to it for my GCSE dance exam and my big crush Mark Nicholson filmed it. I had no idea until I came to the US that Trojan was a make of condoms! Another one of my favourite films *The Breakfast Club* also makes so much more sense now I get the references. 'PB and J with the crusts cut off' is a peanut butter and jelly sandwich (or peanut butter and jam sandwich). I get so excited when things suddenly make sense!

In the same way, this connection with Jax is helping me see myself more clearly in context – my age, my culture and what life experience has taught me so far. So many things he hasn't come across in his life are because he's not old enough to have experienced them yet. I'm enjoying handing over these small 'cheese gives you weird dreams' information bites. I can see that being someone's sexual and life experience guide is going to be a lot of fun.

Jax didn't really wanted to get out of bed, so we lay there in the half-light with him stroking my breasts until he finally peeled himself out of bed chanting the mantra, 'Cupcakes and coffee, cupcakes and coffee.'

I wish he could have stayed and just slept a while longer but I fell right back to sleep once he had gone. He's moving into his new place in a few weekends' time and I know he's keen to make a good impression on his job, so doesn't want to be late or mess up. He told me that he feels like a man finding his own feet in a new town, and I get the sense that he is really proud of himself. I think San Francisco to him feels like a real-time stepping out. I remember having that feeling when I first left the village in Ireland where I'd grown up and moved to London. I moved into this really horrible bedsit with a small cooker that sat on top of the fridge. The whole room was like an oven in summer. A single bed, disgusting decor and a shared bathroom with a resident ginger pubic hair that had its own way of moving towards your mouth when you lay in the deep bath – like a pubic hair with an outboard motor. The odd thing was no one who lived there had ginger hair! But it was my space, right opposite where I worked and paid for with my own wages.

I didn't stay there long and kept upgrading my bedsits until they became 'studios'. When I started teaching English as a foreign language at City Lit, I moved into a much better place and eventually bought a house with my boyfriend at the time, only to buy him out years later when we split up. That was the house I sold to move to San Francisco.

Wednesday 26th January

I've decided to send Jax the script from the zombie movie, as I think the layout might help him with his writing, so I sent him a text asking for his email address. I got a text back. Now I know his surname (cue evil laugh!). Just a small thing that perhaps you should know when you are fucking someone but it isn't so important. What it is good for is Internet stroking. Put it into Google and take a look around. I found him on Facebook. His page was totally open and not private. Sadly it didn't have a photo of him, just a crazy-looking Jesus dude with a mad look in his eyes.

While I was there, I decided to look up the director of that zombie film. He was one of those people you would imagine being a dark recluse film director for the rest of his life. He was always smoking and used to stand hunched over his cigarette, like his brain was so full of existential angst that it would make him fall over one day. Suffering poverty for his art, shagging young actresses who look up to him for his brooding talent. But no, he is married with a baby!!! I don't quite understand how this has happened but I have this feeling that I might be the only person I know left chasing the dream of the glamorous life. By glamorous I mean suffering for my art. I can't believe my sad melancholic, existential anxiety-ridden director has joined the white-picket-fence crew. Fuck, that's kind of impossible. If he's had the sense to end his creative loneliness, am I actually the idiot for still enjoying wallowing in mine?

Everyone grows up. I'm just not sure I did. I still want people to be the way that I preserved them in my thoughts when they were at their coolest. This now makes me super uncool or them fakes. Sometimes I feel like the fake in my own life, maybe I am the only one really living the truth. Or maybe the truth is that we are all fakes.

There wasn't much more about Jax out there in Internet land. He has a MySpace account with some photos on it. It's now said that Facebook is for older people and MySpace for the younger, but at the end of the day Facebook was started by college kids so they could in keep touch with each other and the latest gossip, their likes and comments. It was created to salve the ego of the teens-to-early twenty-somethings and by a culture that is a teenage in its own evolution. Yet this platform has strangely, and almost overnight, become the marker that publishers look at, to see whether your social media popularity makes you worthy of publishing. My publisher Diane is always on about growing my following. The bottom will fall out of it one day when the kids decide it is a load of crap and middle-aged people stop using it as a measure to see if they are aging better than everybody they went to school with. Yet for all of my general self-riotousness about Facebook, here I am using it to stalk a guy I fancy like some ridiculous schoolgirl. I am never going to be part of his life, introduced to his friends or taken home to meet his mom. I used to collect photos and music to remember people by. Now I collect friends and followers on Facebook.

Friday 28th January

My phoned pinged and it was a text from Jax. It read:

> Hey Sam, Thanks for sending over the script. It looks super cool. I love Brit movies and you guys do horror and villains way better. It's the scary accent LOL. Not been so good, all these lates and early mornings catching up with me. Not going to see you so I can do some self-care. Will call you soon. Jx

Don't know why he said 'Call you soon' because we never call, it's always a text. He doesn't pick up the phone when I call him, just lets it go to voicemail then sends me a text – but that's the wonders of the modern age for you. I remember sitting by the phone waiting for Mark to call, the same Mark Nicholson from school that filmed my *Little Red Corvette* dance. Then, if a boy said he would call you, you would wait by the phone. If it rang, you'd leave it ringing three times so it didn't look like you were waiting. But you wouldn't go out. You wouldn't miss that call.

Now people can run late and mess you about all because if they tell you just in advance of being a fucktard, it doesn't make them a fucktard. I think Jax is run down and isn't been a fucktard, but it feels like a blow off.

I know what I have done; the script sending was a step in the direction of being too keen. Freakin' tightrope walking!

Hey Jax, no problem, I have a pretty full on week unfolding with the book and interviews etc. I will make sure I will keep my scary accent in check when delivering some descriptive sexual acts next time you're fucking me. Sam x

Like what? Jx

Like telling you how your hard cock is like catnip to my pussy! Sam x

And…Jx

I want you to tease me with your tongue until I grab you by your ass and beg for it!

I'm starting to feel better. Jx

Tell me what it would take to tempt you to come and see me tonight? I have a few medicinal tricks that I'm sure would make you feel better. Sam x

I'm now suffering from hornyashellitis and my cock is hard but my body is weak. It's not making me feel better, it's worse! Jx

Oh babe, you don't have to worry, I can give you mouth to mouth, while rubbing my wet pants over your stiff cock. Sam x

Not helping, my cock is now throbbing in time with my head. If you keep going it's not the only thing that will be stiff, you'll kill me! Jx

Seriously babe, if you're not feeling well enough to 'cum' over, and I mean all over, then best you stay at home. Sam x

I hate you. Jx

Not cumming then? Sam x

Yes, but sadly only by my own hand. Jx

Waste! Sam x

Sorry! Jx

My book is due out in a few weeks' time, and I am working hard trying to get media attention and book signings. I'm starting to feel a bit less like a fraud having a book on relationships and being single. I am hoping that if I am asked that question in interviews, I'll be able to give the nice easy answer and say, 'I have a lover.'

People still don't see you as successful if you're single. When I was researching the book, I interviewed a professional dominatrix in London. She had some really interesting things to say about spirituality and the dynamics of S&M play. I'm really not into the pain stuff but the idea of role-play, and also meeting a whole community of people who are liberated from sexual conformity, really interests me. She said that being masculine is taking the lead, after all it's the penis that penetrates the vagina and it can't be the other way round. The feminine then has to be submissive.

I can see why dominance and submission is an extreme of those dynamics. It's not a world I have ever really ventured into, except on the few occasions when I've messed around with some Ann Summers' fluffy handcuffs. This is where the guy fucks you in exactly the same way as he usually does, but you're not stretching his back at the time. To be honest I couldn't really see the point if it lacks imagination! I wanted to write about kink in the book to make sure that I covered all of the topics from the perception that you can see everything spiritually.

My dominatrix friend set me up with a meeting with a sex educator in San Francisco. She's also an author, so today I went to meet her to pick her brain about ways to promote my book. We met in a coffee shop called Wicked Grounds, which is based on a place in London called Coffee and Kink. I remembered the place from my teaching days because it was just down the road from where I used to go swimming in a rooftop lido in Covent Garden.

When I walked into the coffee shop, she was already talking with the fetish club owner from *Kitten Control*. She introduced us, but I really wasn't sure if they were having a meeting and whether I should come back later. However, she invited me to sit. He was arranging a date for her to come and give a demonstration at the Pink Party, which I gathered from their conversation, was a meet-and-greet before the fetish club night started. This was to be a special one as it was planned for Valentine's night.

Mistress X then turned to me and said, 'You should come and talk about your book at the Pink Party.'

And before I knew it I had a date in the diary for a book promotion – not quite the type of audience I was expecting, but still a booking. I said yes, of course, while knowing it was a Californian yes – meaning being positive about everything but then cancelling at the last minute, or being late or not showing up! I wouldn't do any of those three things, but I might cancel in plenty of time!

When I got home, I immediately looked up the club and found that some of the rooms were just…well, beds.

When I told Nat about it over wine later, I expected her to laugh but instead she said, 'I've always been curious what it would be like to go to a place like that.'

I couldn't help the surprised expression on my face, but then she said, 'I've heard of that place, I have always wanted to go, but you have to go with a guy and I've never wanted to tell a guy I would wanna go, as he would think I was a slut.'

'You'd go?' I asked.

'Totally! Why not? You're in control. You don't have to do anything you don't want to. You can just walk around and look. Loads of really cool people go to places like that. People with professional jobs that just want a bit of adventure.'

'You mean it's not full of sad old men in grey macs jerking off in corners?'

'No, they wouldn't get in because you have to go with a partner. What really freaks you out about it?'

I thought for a minute and decided to reply honestly, 'That I might like it!'

'What's wrong with that?' Nat asked.

'I'd have to admit to myself that I might just be a dirty perv.'

'What's wrong with that?'

'I like to be a nice girl!'

'And nice girls don't like sex, what planet are you on? What century are you living in? Cut yourself out of the chastity belt Jane Austen!'

'I know, I know, but would you seriously tell a new partner how many men you have slept with, or that you've been to a sex club? That stuff intimidates guys because they don't believe they will measure up and then, to stop themselves feeling sensitive about it, label you a slut. I want to be open with the man I'm in love with, so the less we have to work through from my past the more chance we have of working out.'

'Horse shit!' Nat said decisively.

'Seriously why?'

'Because the right guy won't look at you like that! The right guy would know you have an adventurous spirit. The right guy would love that about you. The right guy would see that you're always curious and wanting more and that the world is amazing. He would love you for who you are! You think *your* right guy has had no life experience? That he hasn't lived in other countries? Not got his own juggernaut of regrets and baggage? You'd never settle for Mr Normal! You'd eat that guy alive and spit out his balls! You'd be better off being your real self, living how you want and staying single.'

I couldn't help laughing at Nat's impassioned speech, 'OK give me a hell yeah!'

'Hell yeah sister, bring on the dancing girls!'

'You're right, you're totally right, Nat! I can't keep

changing myself for someone I haven't met! I'm not seeking sex. I'm seeking experiences. Throwing myself into different environments to learn who I am in each place.'

'That's what life's about, if you have the balls!'

We met up later with a friend of hers called Claire, who I have met a few times, and Nat decided to tell her all about the sex club. Now Claire is a vivacious girl, tall and rounded with a contagious laugh. She wears foundation that would look all right if she had a suntan or if she continued the colour down her neck. As it is, her make-up stops at her jawline, so she looks like Robert Smith from The Cure in tan rather than looking like *The Crow*. She also wears lipstick that matches her clothes perfectly, but doesn't match her face.

From my first impressions of her, I'd say that she's the kind of woman you would dread sitting next to on a flight, but once you got talking you would be having G&T and putting the world to rights. When Nat told her about the sex club – without even glancing over her shoulder, as if it were no confession – she told us that she sees a guy who gives her a massage and makes her cum, if she pays him extra. He calls it a tantric massage. Claire said it's called a 'halloumi', but I've always thought *that* was a Cypriot cheese. The guy won't have sex with her, even though she has asked him and offered to pay more, because he has a girlfriend and that's not part of what he does.

For some reason, I was shocked by her confession and don't know why? I am bewildered that I was so shocked.

I think Claire knew I was shocked too, because she turned to me and said, 'Sweetie, this is America. Nobody holds hands with a fat girl in California. I can get laid, no problem, a guy will stick his cock into a hole in a watermelon. I don't care about getting laid. I want someone to touch me, to enjoy making me cum, to feel my whole body, not just check I'm wet and push it in. I want a boyfriend, but I don't want fat guys. I want cute guys. I want to push my fingertips into muscle not blubber. I can have what I want, I have money!'

She said he charges $150 and offered me his number. Why would I need his number?

Claire told us that she would love to open a sex salon for women just like her. Mostly because she is fed up with being thought of as a slut for wanting to have uncomplicated sex and then, after the uncomplicated sex, wondering why he doesn't return the call for a repeat performance – it just leads to heartache.

But if the only way to rebuild your self-esteem is to have sex, then you lower all kinds of values – and I don't need sex that kills my self-esteem. If the boundary is set by money, it is all the simpler for your emotions and your head. Claire said that there are hundreds of women who would like to have a massage followed by a little extra. She said this guy has lots of clients and she found him on craigslist.

It made me think about how many men I knew who would love to do that job. We both agreed that the salon wouldn't offer intercourse or blow jobs because then the man would be getting off and the whole focus should be on the woman.

The conversation started to feel like we were having a business meeting to confirm the details of how it would work right down to the perfect decor! It made me think of the vibrator play, also known as *In the Next Room* –

I haven't seen it but Anna told me it was on at Berkeley Rep Theater, and said I would love it. It's about women in Victorian times that saw their doctor for emotional problems. The doctor used a vibrator to bring the woman to orgasm and it would cure their depression. This is in a time before they knew about the female orgasm, so apparently they didn't know what they were doing. You bet it would cure a repressed Victorian woman! There must have been a queue through the door!

Claire told us about a gallery opening of erotic art and given it seemed to be the theme of the evening we decided to go.

There were some normal people there and some people dressed in PVC and leather. Whenever I walk into that kind of environment it scares me a bit, so I always walk around like I own the place. But then I like going to nightclubs and pretending that I am Britney Spears who has just walked in with her entourage. I don't know how it works but it makes heads turn!

So I walked in as though I had a hot man on a lead trailing behind me and ended up talking to a photographer whose artworks lined the walls. I tried to make some artistic small talk, so that it would sound like I could see the artistic value in his creations. So I talked about how the hand in the bottom right of the photo was more erotic than the girl bent over with her glistening bum in the air. I cleverly, and with great knowledge and artistic flair, told him that the hand looked as if it was the one controlling element that turned the photo from porn to art.

In response he smiled and nodded.

Encouraged I went on and asked him what inspired

him. He told me the hand was an accident. It got in the way of the shot and that he picks models that he would like to fuck.

Totally flummoxed I said, 'That's a bit unprofessional.'

'Only if I fuck them and, at that point, I don't care about what's professional if they say yes.'

I seamlessly but swiftly moved on to the red velvet homemade cupcakes where the girls were huddled and shortly afterwards we left.

Drinking more wine, we laughed ourselves silly about the photographer. Nat thought I should have asked him if he needed a new model and then if he'd said no, said, 'How about a fuck then?'

He was really nasty! Claire reckoned his success rate might be quite high.

Today has been one of those surreal days, which is quite often the case in San Francisco. Everything that is normally covered up has been talked about. It seems that if you're not bisexual then you need therapy for being repressed!

At home I sent a text to Jax.

How are you feeling? Sam x

Tell me sexy stuff to make me feel better? Jx

You and me in a dark bar. We find a corner and you run your hand up the inside of my thigh, over my clit through my wet silk pants then withdraw just as the waitress in a short skirt goes by, and I have to win your attention back. What should I do? Sam x

Fuck the waitress I wouldn't stop. I'd take you up against the wall faster and harder if there was an audience. Jx

You'd like that? Sam x

Dunno, never done it. Maybe the film director in me would like an audience. Jx

I could be under the table massaging you with my mouth as people walked by, totally oblivious to how close you are to cumming. Sam x

I'd want you on the table on all fours while everyone was watching. Jx

I see you're feeling better. Sam x

Still super tired, but weird and can't sleep, even knocking out a hand job isn't helping. Jx

Babe, I hope you get some rest tonight. Sam x

Thanks, I'll call you when I'm feeling better. Jx

Why say call, he doesn't 'do' calling!

Saturday 29th January

I had one of my recurring dreams last night. When I was a child, I often used to dream about a child who was my double and would come out of a mirror. In the dream, I'd run down a corridor through some fire doors and past gilt mirrors until I found the right mirror. Then my double would jump out of the mirror and come on a journey with me.

Those dreams stopped when I chose to hang out in dreamland with the actor who played Robin in *Robin of Sherwood* rather than her.

The next morning my period started. That's when the flying dreams started and I'd fly over the tops of the houses. I could lift myself off the ground with an energy force that came from my solar plexus. I always felt disappointed in the morning when I couldn't really fly.

And then there are the Mark Nicholson dreams, which I've had since I lost touch with him in my early twenties. Mark was the guy I wish I had lost my virginity to. Well, it wasn't so much about him but about a situation I was in with him, where I let my head rule my heart. I even wrote about that evening in my book. We never dated, snogged a few times at school discos, but he was my first earth-shattering crush. There was such a strong pull between the two of us, I felt like he travelled inside of me. He wasn't into me and I kind of fell over myself constantly trying to get his attention. But we were kids and that's kind of what happens. Over the years I have looked for him in social media, but I'm not sure why because the last I heard was that he'd got married and had a kid.

If I'm honest, I find the dreams about him disturbing and wonder if they are holding me back from being in a real relationship with someone else. Needless to say, I have analysed them from every angle, hoping that they hold a key to something important. The theme is always the same, we are going to have sex in the dream, but we never do. How this all comes about is different every time and what stops us having sex is different every time. It normally involves other people turning up or getting in the way. In the dream, I remember the dreams and I tell him that I've had recurring dreams about him for years. In the dream, he seems less than interested in this fact. I wonder if I were to ever find him and tell him about the dreams, would the dreams stop coming?

In this last dream we were at his parents' house and we are talking upstairs while his family, including his child are downstairs. We are sitting on the bed and I am telling him about the dream and how he has continued to age along with me, no matter that I haven't seen him for twenty years. Of course, he always looks sexy, didn't get bald or fat, but that's the thing about dreams! I somehow know we are going to have sex, even though in the dream he doesn't kiss me. But he has to go downstairs and I am left sitting at the bottom of the bed wondering how long I should wait for him and then I wake up. In some of the dreams we make out, and even though I can remember how he kisses as if it was yesterday, but in the dreams he has a kind of snake tongue that flicks, and not in a good way!

I had a 'kitchen conversation' with Anna about it this morning. She has a great way of making coffee. She has a pot where you put water in the bottom and coffee in the top, then the stream rises and fills the top with beautifully made coffee. She told me it's Spanish and can't believe that even though I'm from Europe I have never used one.

Anna is an actress and I found her post for a flatmate on craigslist. She wanted to sublet her room for a month while she was performing a show out of town. Sitting in my house in London, I knew it would be the perfect place. It would give me the chance to move over to San Francisco and start college, find my feet and then somewhere to live. I planned to go back and collect the dog from my mum's once I was settled.

The flat had two other guys living there at the time, one was a lawyer with the most incredible laugh and the other was a shop assistant – and they were not getting along. Matt felt Keir was too noisy late at night, Anna was sorry that I was moving into a disrupted house but it worked to my advantage because it was Keir's being so loud and acting like a child when you told him to be quiet that finally got him kicked out, which meant I was able to take his room permanently. We then convinced the landlord to let the dog move in too.

The flat is really big, with a long corridor, which the dog just loves being able to run down playing fetch with a ball. Anna is an amazing sounding board, and thinks my Mark dreams are about missed opportunities. She's told me to tell her when I have one so we can mark it up against what's going on in my waking life. She might just be right as I've always lived my life in fear of not having done enough with it and having regrets. It's a repeated theme in my life and this is a recurring dream, so maybe that's it.

Tuesday 1st February

The first copy of my book arrived today. I was in the flat on my own when the UPS man came to the door. Our UPS man is really cute, even dressed in the shit-brown uniform that matches the truck – who thought that was a good idea? Is it so they can hide themselves in safety against the side of the truck, if something arrives broken? Perfectly camouflaged, they can slip along the side of the van and into the driving seat and make a quick getaway. Maybe that's why the driver's door is missing! I often see him when I am out with the dog and I'm sure he leans over the passenger seat deliberately so I can look at his pert ass in those tight brown pants. He then smiles and his thick bushy black handlebar 'tashe makes his teeth gleam white, as if they have one of those cheesy toothpaste ads white flash tings. He hands me the book in a brown Jiffy bag, which matches everything else. I rip open the corner and see the edge of the cover. I then have to clean the whole flat, rearrange my room and take the dog round Dolores Park three times before I can open it.

When I do, the smell of new book between the pages is intoxicating. As an English teacher, I am a lover of language and just seeing all of the words across the pages, knowing they are my own, gives me a thrill. I have always loved the smell of a new book, but when that book is your own it has an extra edge of arousal to it. I flick through the pages, diving in to read odd parts of it, trying to find something that will make me cringe or feel delighted. Here in the pages is the leadership voice of an instructive author. Someone you can feel safe with and trust in their opinion. Perhaps one thing about having a list of relationships that haven't worked means that it does leave you more of an expert in relationships than the people who have only had one successful one. Just for starters, you know that not all people are the same.

A wave of feeling hits me and suddenly I feel sure that *I can do* the necessary marketing. Writing a book is one of the most vulnerable things you can do. It's really exposes who you are as a person because once it's printed you can't change your mind. Which means if your mind expands and you learn new things that counter the things you once believed, you are still known for what you once said. Writing a book is like getting a literary mind tattoo, once it's in ink, you can't decide that you don't like it later; it's done for life. With a book that's possibly even longer than your life.

On top of that, you have to sell it. You go from being alone in a room being an introvert during its creation, to being thrown into being an extrovert for its launch. Having to stick your neck out and market it feels like an act of cruelty. Holding the book now, like a newborn baby, I am willing to give it the start in life it needs to flourish.

I want to share this moment with Jax. Well, in fact, I want to share this moment with anyone who will be just as excited as I am. That wasn't going to be Jax, he wasn't here and it also felt a bit needy. I have always prided myself on not being needy, but then wondered why all the needy, nagging girls get the guy! So I couldn't call him and say 'Hey make a big fuss of me, I've had this big thing happen and now I'm having a big wobble and need a hug.'

Oh God, I need a hug and the absence of having the person who would give a shit reduces me to feeling lonely. Jax said he would get in touch when he was feeling better but I know he has his house move coming up too. Being new in town, I don't know who he has to help him move if he is too exhausted to do it. So, I sent him a text.

Hey Jax, how are you doing? How's the move going?
Sam x

Good, all done, don't own Jack shit. Jx

What are you up to tonight? Sam x

Might see my cousin for some beers. I'll let you know later. Jx

OK, let me know. Sam x

For the rest of day I kept busy. I made a list of independent bookshops and sex shops in San Francisco then printed some flyers and took them round to each place, each time asking to speak to the book buyer. Sometimes I got lucky and other times they just took the flyer and said if it matched their product list they would stock it. Of course I could have sent them a press release by email, but it's much harder to ignore a face.

Then I went back home and sent a follow-up press release asking them if they would like a copy of the book.

There is an interesting thing about sales psychology, if you see something three times, no matter where you saw it, even it's Facebook, Twitter and a newspaper you will think it's popular. So I turn up with a flyer, follow them on Twitter and Tweet the book cover then I send them the press release and hope I have hit enough buttons that they starting thinking they've heard of this book because it's popular. It is a lot of work, but that's the job.

There is a sex shop at the end of our road called Good Vibrations. I went in there and was confronted by a very beautiful girl covered in tattoos and body piercings. She told me that many of the vibrators are not that good for women. I already knew that the vagina was the most absorbent part of the body and there are health benefits in having sex with the same partner and absorbing their sperm through the walls of the vagina – no baby required. I looked into this phenomenon for the book, as I was recommending the cap (also known as the diaphragm) as the best form of contraception outside of condoms. But I had never even considered that all the chemicals, plastic and rubber that are used to make vibrators could also be absorbed into the body via the vagina. It made sense though as there is a real chemical smell when you unwrap a new vibrator – a bit like when you first drive a new car. She told me they were harmful if you are exposed to them a lot. Like tampons, vibrators can cause toxic shock syndrome. Things intended for the vagina don't have the same restrictions as food, and yet we absorb them both into the body.

Needless to say, I wasn't that surprised when she told me there was a solution, which they stocked, of course – a brand new environmentally friendly and non-toxic vibrator.

It was orange, although I have no idea why they thought it was the best colour for a vibrator. Good visibility in the dark, perhaps? Once she showed me the various functions, settings and speeds, I wanted it. Now I knew the truth, I knew that it would be impossible to ever trust my good and rather old toxic vibrator again. She had just squashed all the pleasure out of any masturbatory experience between my old faithful and me. If any other thought enters my head while I'm mid-climax, the orgasm stops. For example, you might be an amazing lover, but if a woman thinks for a moment that she's left the oven on or the back door unlocked, then her build goes and you have to start from the top. So in the height of pleasure, if I suddenly think...*I wonder if this vibrator is safe* then BOOM it's all over for the bunnies in the pleasure palace!

Having bought the vibrator, she then tried to sell me strawberry-flavoured lube, which completely destroyed her argument and left me wondering whether I had just been conned. But it was said in a kind of 'want fries with that' fast food kind of way, and I was just grateful that she didn't ask me if I wanted to 'go large'!

Hey Sam, my cousin is out with his girl, I'm hungry, wanna get some food? Jx

I met Jax outside the Roxie Theater on 16th and took him to my favourite Vietnamese restaurant next door. The food at this place is just amazing. You can see right into the kitchen, which just looks like cooking chaos. The waiting staff are really horrible and exceptionally rude, even by British standards so by American standards they might as well be spitting in your food. Yet the place is always packed because the food is so good, really cheap and they pump the smells from the kitchen right out on to the street, so you can't help but get drawn in. I often feel totally intimidated in this place but with Jax there, I felt more confident. We watched the tables as the staff growled at the customers, which seem to make the customers all the nicer.

Jax said, 'You know what it is?'

I put my head on one side, to make a question.

'Guilt!' He announced, like it was the most obvious answer.

'Oh, of course, don't mention the war – "now I've said it once and I think I got away with it".'

Jax didn't get the *Fawlty Towers* reference, but agreed.

I had been to Vietnam when I was travelling. I must be a bit morbid because I visited to the war museum three times. I wanted to go until I didn't find it shocking anymore. I still can't understand how humans could do that to each other. I told him about it, and Jax asked me lots of questions. I told him about the pickled babies in jars that show the effects of napalm and chemical weapons. I told him that I couldn't decide whether I was more shocked by the disfigured babies or the fact they were pickled in jars, as if they weren't even human.

'Did you meet any Americans there?' he asked.

'Well, I did take one American guy, who was staying in the same place as me, with me on my last visit to the museum. When we came out, I expected some kind of horror or emotional connection, but he simply said, "That place is totally bias".'

'No fucking way!' Jax said.

I enjoyed talking to him about it, and it made me

think about the date with Rick – the biker, smiley-face, ex-boyfriend-clone guy – when I said that most people don't want to hear about your stories and experience. Perhaps Jax does because he still has his whole life ahead of him. He still has time to do all of these things, so the tales of my adventures give him ideas rather than make him jealous over something he hasn't done.

On the way back to the flat, I tell him about my super non-toxic environmentally friendly vibrator. We laughed about how I am going to recycle the old one. In San Francisco they check through your bins to make sure you're recycling correctly and fine the landlord if you aren't. I had visions of my landlord who lives on the top floor getting a letter about my vibrator with its smiling face knob end not being out in the 'plastics'. Would it be classed as plastic...or rubber? Jax asked why the knob end was smiling. Apart from the ridiculous answer of 'Wouldn't you smile if your main job was pleasuring a woman', there was a practical one.

'It was made in Japan,' I told him, 'and in the time of the Shogun, craftsmen were forbidden to create dildos in the shape of a cock. To get around this law the craftsmen carved a face on the end. I believe the law still stands to this day. Hence my vibrator sported a smiley.' I told him triumphantly while trying not to laugh.

Jax went quiet for a while and I realised I must sound as if I know something about everything and that might be quite intimidating. I hope he's not put off. I decide not to tell him I have the book as that might really tip it. But no, he wasn't thinking any of that and piped up, 'Can I see the vibrators?'

'Of course!' I said happily and left him with my box

of tricks, while I took the dog out. Actually there wasn't much in there. I'd left most of it in the UK because I didn't want to risk being searched by US customs. When I got back to the bedroom Jax had unwrapped the new one and inserted the batteries.

'Let's go for a test drive.' He said, grinning.

Kissing me, he peeled off my clothes and lay me down on the bed. Placing the vibrator in my hand, he said, 'Show me.'

A thrilling rush ran through me as the cool silicone touched my wet pussy. I turned it on, starting with a slow buzz on the clit massager running it round in circles to get my clit standing to attention. As I did Jax filled my mouth with his tongue, deeply fucking me with it. It made me want him inside me, but it was too soon for that. So I inserted the larger end of the vibrator. It isn't like a penis; it is curved to hit the G-spot rather than deep penetration. My hips rose to meet my hand as I started fucking myself with it. Jax stopped kissing me to watch. The intensity of his intrigue turned me on even more and it became a kind of performance. Once he was sure he knew what I was doing. He took over the vibrator with one hand and tweaked my nipples with the other. The rush ran over my body like a pinball hitting my erogenous zones and set off desire lights in my brain. My orgasm started to build, but Jax kept slowing down my hips with a gentle hand as I tried to grind harder into the vibrator.

'I'm not ready to let you cum yet,' he said and every so often made a 'shush' sound, which soothed my arousal and made me relax again onto the bed. He found another button on the vibrator, which I hadn't realised, made the curved cock part vibrate, and as he slowly turned up the speed I thought my pleasure would explode through the roof. His hand stroked my body, squeezing my breasts, scratching my thighs. All of these movements taking a little away from the intensity of desire coming from my pussy. He kept fucking me with the vibrator while he used his tongue on my really hard clit. I took a moment to watch him, but then the waves started coming in too close a succession. My head rolled back and I made sounds I didn't even recognise as being me. With my eyes closed, the black on the back of my eyelids seemed to stretch out forever. I lost all identity and became completely wrapped in the moment. My body seemed to disappear as all I could feel was the extreme sensation coming from my pussy, which seemed to stretch out into the whole universe. I couldn't fight it, to keep hold of myself. I felt at one with everything and such an extreme sensation of love pouring out of me started from between my pubic bones and ran right through the core of my body. My breathing was in direct rhythm to the thrusting of the vibrator. The levels of ecstasy mounted, but still I hadn't climaxed and was way beyond the feeling of pleasure I normally have before I peak. I knew I had to let go, but it felt a little scary.

As if he knew Jax said, 'You're safe I've got you, baby,' and with that the whole universe seemed to crack open, like I was held in a bubble of the most unconditional love. A roar came from my mouth and with it I felt like I had let go fully. I was released and open. Tears came from my eyes, even though I was the happiest and most relaxed I have ever felt; my whole body jumped at the slightest touch. Jax turned off the vibrator and held me. His arms around me, his smell was reassuring but I still felt really vulnerable. After all he hadn't done this with me, he had done it too me!

'That was amazing,' he said, kissing my ear 'you're amazing.'

I felt, wet, chilled and small, and yet at the same time as if some kind of miracle had just happened. After a while just lying there together, still and in an almost in a meditative blissed-out place, he asked how I was doing. I tried to talk, but just didn't have the voice. He handed me some water and I became aware of the sounds I must have made to make my voice hoarse. Taking the water back from me and putting it on the side, he ran his hands over the inside of my thighs, which were wet. I was still sensitive but not as much. He then moved down to my vagina and started licking all of it, outside the lips, inside the lips, big tongue lapping away at me and it felt amazing. He must have got the condom when he picked up the water because suddenly he pulled up from licking me and pushed the tip of his cock a little into me. I had cum so hard that my stomach was still in knots and I wasn't sure if I could now have sex with him. He pushed in a little more, and asked, 'Are you ready?'

My hips did the talking and I pushed up to greet his cock. He moved slowly and pulled himself up higher, so he was angled perfectly to rub my G-spot. Moving slowly while he kissed me, our bodies felt like one. I could feel that sensation of love coursing between the two of us and I knew for the first time in all of this crazy sex with him, we were making love. I could feel every inch of his cock as he pulled out right to the tip and then slowly pushed down to the base and pushed into my cervix. Then with lighter smaller mini thrusts the head of his cock focused on my

G-spot alone before going in deep again. I was in rapture, wave after wave of pleasure until I had the sweetest little G-spot orgasm, which seemed to crop up on me from out of nowhere.

Jax had to push in harder to stop the tightness of my pussy forcing him out and then took me for himself. He pushed a pillow under my bum and focused on his orgasm. I was grateful for the pillow as it meant I could just lie back and take it, without having use my stomach muscles to push upwards. He raised my legs so they were on his chest and started to fuck me deeply, which I loved but was just too much to take. I felt trapped under his body as he used me for his own pleasure.

You deserve this you little bitch, I thought to myself as his fucking speed increased to match his building. *Hang in there!* I thought. I grabbed his ass and he filled my mouth with his tongue again, and I felt consumed totally by him. Then his head rolled back and he gave one, two, three final deep thrusts then shot his cum into me. He let my legs drop and I could almost immediately feel how much of a rag doll my body had become. There wasn't an ounce of tension left in me and I knew this feeling would last for a week.

We fell asleep in each other's arms without even going to the bathroom for a clean up. He woke up before the alarm. I didn't hear him until he was at the door.

'See you later, cupcake,' he said as he closed it.

Cupcake! He was clearly thinking about work! I fell back to sleep.

Friday 4th February

I have spent the last few days on a real high and walking like a cowboy. My legs don't seem to close properly, like a door not fully on its hinges. I'm convinced that everyone can see that I am walking funny. I went to a yoga class yesterday to try and reopen my hips, as everything feels so tight, but it didn't help that stretched feeling in my inside legs. It's a nice feeling but a constant reminder of sex, and it's making it hard to focus on the other stuff I have to do.

Nat and I took a drive out to Muir Woods to see the redwood trees. They are so enormous and the place is so beautiful it was really breathtaking. It's amazing how different Nat and I are when we are out in nature. Not talking so much, leaving loads of space and just slowing down. It's like getting back in touch with yourself.

I asked Nat why she had never had kids.

She thought for a moment and then said, 'You know secretly, I don't believe I can be the mother I want to be and get all my shit done. I'm scared I would be like one of those yelling moms or I would have to give up on my goals. My life is already all out of whack with working so hard for the rent. Did you know there are more people with dogs in San Francisco than have kids?'

'I didn't know that. Why?'

'Well when you have kids you have to move into the

suburbs as it's impossible to raise kids in a tiny flat and most people can't afford anything bigger. Then there is the medical insurance. I wouldn't even know where to start with all that.'

'Do you feel like you're missing out, Nat?'

'Not really,' she replied. 'You can feel all that love without having your own children. What about you?'

'I think I'm going to be a wicked step-mum to someone else's kids, I mean wicked in a good way. Best of both worlds, you get to love them, play with them, support them and they're not your responsibility. I could then get on with my work and also be a beautiful part of a child's life.'

'That's all very romantic until you meet his ex who hates you!'

'I had forgotten that they usually come with an ex, but we might get on great and go on family holidays.'

Nat stopped walking and looked at me, 'Seriously?'

'I learnt a lot about my capacity to be a mum when I got a dog. I never thought I would be able to handle my sleep being interrupted, but if she needs to go out or hears something and barks, I'm so fine with it all!'

We carried on walking for a while in silence and I wondered if I had triggered something in Nat or if she was thinking that she'd be a terrible mother and I haven't the heart to tell her. So I burst back from the silence with some cultural insights.

'I believe children need a community, like it used to be when we lived close to our whole families, grandparents, cousins, aunties and uncles. In Ireland if I got caught doing something bad, I'd hear "I know your mother". Then you'd get a clip and be told, "That's from her". If I came home and told my mum some stranger hit me then she would clip me round the ear and say, "Why, what were you doing?" I felt safe having those boundaries.'

'What's a clip?' Nat asked.

'Like a light smack round the side of the head.'

'You'd get sued for that here.'

We stopped off for a drink at Cavallo Point on the way back and looked at the Golden Gate Bridge through the trees. The nice bartender, that Nat had given her card to last time we were there, wasn't working. I showed Nat the book and she was suitably impressed.

Then she asked, 'Have you read that book *He's Just Not That Into You?*'

OK, now I was irritated and a bit hurt, so I told her, 'Nat, that's such a shocking thing to do to an author: look at their book and then start talking about another book. It's like talking about another lover after sex.'

'No, I didn't mean it like that, I was thinking about you and Jax. You should read that book. I think it's written in a style that you'd like. It's really funny.'

'It's called, *He's Just Not That Into You*, and I should read it about Jax? I don't know, I don't think I have to read it. Why don't I just ask you what you think?' I asked her crossly.

'I'm not saying that Sam! I'm just saying it's a really great book.'

We drove back over the Golden Gate Bridge and Nat opened the sunroof so I could take photos. It really is something to see but my favourite landmark of San Francisco is a mast tower on one of the hills. The fog billows down from it and it stands strong through the fog. I'm sure to most people it's just a massive ugly mobile phone mast or something, but I really love it. I've taken more photos of that mast in different coloured skies than I have of the Golden Gate Bridge. The mast is also closer to home.

The book push is all going well, I feel confident about the radio shows now and have been writing some amazing blogs. But Nat's comments cut me to the quick. Mostly because it's clearly true. I have a sex craving for Jax and, while I am trying not to be emotionally needy, I'm chewing the covers! I'd just love to prove Nat wrong about him. But if I am honest, she isn't wrong. So I sent Jax one of those texts when you say it's all about them and your concern for them, but that's a total contact excuse. Everyone knows it but everyone plays along, as one day they will use it too, here's how it went:

Hey Jax

(Using the word 'Hey' at the start of a text or email to make it casual, like a loose raise of the hand. Texting 'Hi' is a frantic wave!)

Wondering what you're up to?

(Wondering, I'm just a bit bored, thinking – I'm just a bit neurotic.)

How are you feeling? Sleeping well?

(It's all about you!)

Just wondering, how the move is going?

(When do I get a shag at your place?)

Sam xx

Seamless and he replied almost immediately.

Not great, if only my worries were health ones, I've got some financial shit going on. Jx

I think that was a weird thing for him to write. If you don't have your health then you don't have anything, but in America your health relies on your wealth. You have to have health insurance to be able to see a doctor. I'm not surprised that Jax is finding it hard to pay the rent. Paying rent in San Francisco is the most I have ever spent anywhere I have lived. For a room in a shared flat, I am paying as much as I did for my mortgage on a two-bedroom house with a garden in London. Being on barista's wages must have made it difficult to raise the deposit, and now I know more about the Tenderloin I wish he didn't live there. I can't have him move in with me because that would be totally crazy. I don't think my flatmates would go for that.

I don't know why it feels like MY problem. In fact, it was an odd thing for him to text –almost as if it were the stream of consciousness going through his head at that moment. I wrack my brain trying to come up with a sympathetic response. It's really hard to know what to say in that kind of situation, except, 'That sucks? I'm sorry to hear that? I can lend you ten bucks.'

Then another text comes in.

If you could make use of a sex slave or houseboy let
me know. Jx

That's funny, I think. Then a cold sense of realisation
comes over me...*Is he joking?*

Thinking about it, I realise that he probably isn't
joking and feel a flurry of sexual intrigue and excitement.
Then I feel sad. Does he see me as being so old that I should
pay him to have sex with him? It's an odd feeling being
insulted and excited at the same time.

I don't want to but I have to I call Nat about Jax's text,
just in case I am missing the punch line of some cultural
joke. I need a second opinion before I text back. Of course,
I don't like the second opinion.

'Oh my God, he has been playing you this whole time!
He's got you hooked in and now you're all loved up, he
wants to charge you for sex! Wow, this boy is something
else, tell him to fuck off!'

I can't have got him that wrong! Can't believe that
it was a shark in the bar New Year's Eve waiting for a
sad-faced old cow with cash! Well if that were the case he
wouldn't have chosen a dive bar. I couldn't text back for a
while; I needed time to think.

I just don't know how I feel. I want to be the person
who can roll with the punches. But I can't work out if
what I am thinking and feeling is based on me and him,
and what I know of him and me to be true, or of society.
I mean role-play and dynamics, it's always the woman with
the sugar daddy, but why not the guy? Why can't he get paid
for sex? Where is my ego coming from on this one? Maybe

this isn't even about me, maybe it is about him. This is a cry for help, which has left me wondering how to get myself out of the way here so I can think about him?

I also know that after asking this question nothing is going to be the same again. I can either pay to see him or be offended and let him go. I'm not offended, in a sense to me this kind of sums up the States. It makes total sense to take advantage of what you've got in order to make money. It's a method of survival that the British don't really understand. If you don't have money in the UK, you're unlikely to die because of it. You're unlikely to be left out in the cold because you don't have health insurance. You're unlikely to end up on the street homeless because you don't have a job. In the US all of these things are possible. You think twice before calling an ambulance for someone in case you're left with the bill for the police, fire service and ambulance that all turn up and charge a $100 each for the privilege.

How must I look to Jax? Maybe I come across as a middle-class woman with lots of money. Maybe he's just chancing his luck because he feels like he's run out of options.

I know I have to reply to the text quickly otherwise it will look like I am upset. Shall I make a joke of it or make it serious? I had sold my house so I can afford it, but it depends on how much money he wants. But how will I feel paying someone to fuck me? And how will he feel once the 'thing' has made him a whore?

I've decided that I need more time, so have sent him a text asking him to meet me tonight for a business meeting. That means I can decide between now and then. He writes back to say that he likes the sound of that.

That afternoon I have time to think. Gripping a copy of my book, I ponder how Jax could be my partner at the book launch. With him on my arm, it would make me look like a freaking guru! I think about the fetish club and how protected I would be if I were there with him when I give my talk at the Pink Party. I think about how in San Francisco, I feel like a fish out of water with all these sexually liberated people – like thinking you're not an alcoholic until surrounded by non-drinkers! I thought I was liberated until I met what liberation looks like. I love the idea of showing Jax the world, buying him clothes, taking him to expensive restaurants. I won't have to compromise; we can do everything I want to. I start to get wet thinking about paying him at the end of each night. The money resting inside the top pocket of his shirt next to his nipple, the weight of the cash pulling his shirt down so I can see the hair on his chest, and even though he has the money, he wants to come home and fuck me. The idea of being in control turns me on.

Jax comes to the house, late of course. We go out right away with the dog to the Dalva. The bar is dark and candlelit. I love this bar; it's right next door to the Roxy Cinema and the Vietnamese place where we had dinner the other night. The bar plays old black-and-white movies projected onto a wall. But for some reason it always smells of chlorine, which totally kills the rest of the ambience. Some nights the smell is stronger than others, but tonight it isn't so bad.

We are both really nervous. I have decided that I don't want to pay for sex. He has decided that he doesn't want to be paid. Bingo!

'I've got no talents,' he said 'and figure that I'm just a twenty-one-year-old-guy with a dick.'

I'm shocked and can't keep it out of my voice, 'That's not true you just might not have found all your talents.'

'Got no money-making talents that's for sure.'

It makes me wonder if that's how a woman feels when she steps into becoming a prostitute. How can you believe that your greatest commodity is being young and having a dick? He is so much more than that. Every person is so much more than that. Our conversation is intimate, and he tells me that he has no guy friends to talk to and, since his cousin dropped him in favour of his girlfriend's wishes, he's feeling really alone. It was, however, his cousin's idea that I pay him for sex.

I tell him that from now on when we go out I will pay for everything. It's not because he hasn't got any money but because I want to pay for everything. I want to show him that he is valuable, so valuable, that just to spend time with him is worth paying for. I'm not sure he understands, but maybe on a deeper level he does. I make it sound very playful so he doesn't feel less of a man. But what he really needs is some male support around him, so I ask about his dad.

He tells me that he lives in California but a long drive away and admits that he's not that close to him as he took his mom's side during the split. He clearly thinks a lot of his dad, but ended up trying to protect the weaker party as he felt that is what he had to do as the only other man.

'You would really like him,' he said. 'In fact you should meet him, I know he would really fancy you, and maybe you two would get together,' he said smiling as though this was a brilliant idea.

The elevator in my chest dropped down from the heart floor into the pit of my stomach. His dad is twenty years older than me, same age gap but in a different direction!

Changing the subject I tell him that I want to buy him clothes, take him to fancy places and get to do whatever I want to do, and pay him for coming with me. I tell him I want him to act like my loving boyfriend at book events too.

He likes the idea of all of it. I like the idea too. It's the kind of thing you'd expect an older man to do for a younger woman. It makes me feel like I am playing the role of Richard Gere in *Pretty Woman*, without the sex being paid for – and sadly without the piano scene.

I tell Jax about the Pink Party, and how I am too scared to go alone, and that I would like to pay him to be my escort. I explain to him that in my fantasy head these clubs seem really exciting but, in reality, I'm a bit of a whimpering Chihuahua.

He tells me that he is a very good protector of other people, and says he will make a very good go-between between the world and me.

Listening to him makes me think of the talks I've given in London, where at the end the audience move forwards, towards me, and not out through the door. I remember when one of my students was up on stage with me and totally panicked when he saw the sea of people coming towards us. I know I come across as being a strong confident person and half of me is, but the other half is just plain scared.

In relationships too, I attract men who are attracted to strong confident women and it feels great to be able to confess the other side of me – even if it's just in conversation.

Jax telling me that he can hold that side of me allows me to breathe out just in that moment. I think all women biologically look for a man who they think can hold them. Can hold their strength, can hold their anger, can hold their vulnerability and don't wig out about holding their hand.

Pretty Woman is now stuck in my head and I decide that I want to take Jax clothes shopping. Watch him be waited on. He loves that idea and I realise that I have never even done that for myself. I guess I've never thought it was worth the money. I tell him I have never spent that kind of money on myself.

'Hey Sam, I'd be happy to be taken to Goodwill and do the fantasy there.'

That warms my heart, because it feels to me that he is more into making me happy than getting a whole load of free clothes. I guess what I'm playing out with him is how I would like to be treated. So maybe what you send out into the universe you receive.

Jax has an incredible ability to make other people want to make him happy. An actor in his soul, he tells me that he feels he could play these roles for me. But, as he says it, I begin to wonder if he's ever actually been himself, or if he knows who that even is.

His wages only cover his rent and nothing more. I am to be his other job so that he can have some spending money. He doesn't want to get a second job, which would mean he'd have to work waiting tables in the evenings. He wants to be able to have that time to write and create, he just doesn't want to have to work all the time and that be his life.

I really don't want to spend my house savings like

this. In fact I need them for my future. But in my present, having Jax in my life is inspiring and exhilarating – I get more done and feel happier. People pay in all kinds of ways and do all kinds of things for that feeling. Our arrangement is of mutual benefit.

He is a little freaked out by the club idea but open to it. In fact I'm a little freaked out by the idea. But aware that I have only scratched the surface of it and want to delve deeper in a safe and protected way. It will also be wonderful to have him on my arm at the book launch. I'm not selling anything that isn't true; it's just that I wouldn't want anyone to know that I am paying for it. In fact, I can't believe I'm in a place in my life where I am prepared to pay for company. However, I think, looking back, that I have I paid for it all my life. Just in different ways in different gifts. It sometimes involved money, it sometimes involved sex, it sometimes involved doing things other people wanted, that I didn't. This connection with Jax feels the most authentic and that feels good. He tells me that he has taken down much of the act he's been putting on for me. Like I couldn't see that mask already.

We decide that if we are going to have sex it is because we both want it. My God after, all of that, do I want to!

As soon as we get into my bedroom, he takes my face in his hands and starts kissing me really tenderly. We drop off our clothes piece by piece and not once do we stop kissing. Moving under the covers, he runs his hand up my leg from my knees, reaching my wetness and pushing me open with his fingers. His tongue pushes deeply into my mouth and I suck it in a little more. Moving backwards and forwards he fucks my mouth with his tongue, making me desperately want his cock inside me. Taking the condoms from the drawer, I slip one on him. He is so hard that he seems even bigger than the times before. His fingers never stop circling my clit and I can feel the waves of my orgasm starting to build. I don't want to wait for that, I want him inside me and as soon as possible. He draws me down onto my back, leveraging himself on top of me, supported by one arm, as he uses the other hand to guide in his cock. I am wet but not quite so engorged and tight so it slips in.

This isn't like the sex that we've had before, this is tender and loving, he kisses my face, neck, breasts, making each entrance slow and deep. He is raised slightly above me so, as his cock drives down, it grinds past my G-spot with every thrust. Every time he pushes in, I grip the muscles of my vagina around him. He groans but doesn't increase his speed. I feel like each time more of him is being sucked into me. He lifts my legs and wraps them round his torso and raises his angle more. He is now so deep it is almost painful, but a very good pain, my orgasm comes on suddenly and with a huge bout of force. My hands grab at his back, my head rolls back, my mouth opens, as I can't stop myself from crying out as the waves of bliss ravage my body.

I feel completely electric, and every small move he makes causes my body to jump and convulse. It makes me laugh and is kind of embarrassing but he really loves it and at odd times strokes my leg. He unwraps my legs from round his back and places them upright on his chest. Very pleased with myself, I know *that* little move is thanks to all those years of being a yoga teacher. Now moving his cock slowly he starts sucking my toes, he starts with the big toe and sucks it in the same way that I like to suck his cock.

Watching him is beautiful, and my body is so fully turned on, my toe feels as sensitive as a dick.

Something changes in his eyes and he looks at my breasts pushed up together between my legs. It is as if a hunger is coming out of his soul through his eyes. Moving my legs back down, I curl them round his back again and this time use my heels on his ass to drive his thrusts. He makes one single growl as he comes, before falling down onto me and wrapping his arms around me. He holds me, cock still inside, my face nuzzled into his neck. We lie there feeling each other breathe. Not moving, just holding on.

I know there are all sorts of chemicals such as oxytocin in a moment like this. But at that moment I knew I was lost. I knew I could feel love, and that last time was so intense I became addicted to him. I felt his breathing change and his body relax onto mine as he fell asleep. I held him there, like I was healing him. It felt like a private moment between his soul and mine. He started dreaming, but woke up when he jumped in his sleep. He moved off me, set the alarm on his phone, pulled me onto his chest and fell back to sleep.

Saturday 5th February

I decided to make our first 'business' meeting very simple. I sent Jax a text message with his first assignment, to take me to the cinema. Nothing heavy at all, I will pay for the evening and give him some cash at the end of it. I told him that my chosen movie is *Legion*, he wrote back:

> Angel Wars. Love it. Meet you there @ 7 on Thursday evening then? If something comes up I'll let you know well in advance. Jx

> Great, we can play hunt the popcorn in a popcorn bucket without a bottom. Sam x

> Oh no doubt you'll find that popcorn. Jx

It's a bit like buying a Lottery ticket. I don't believe I will win, but I pay a pound to dream about winning and to make plans with what I would do with the money if I won. Paying Jax is far better. For the whole time since sending that message I have been fantasizing. I wake up in the morning thinking about it. I can't get it out of my head because I'm thinking about it. The difference is that I will get my fantasy. Maybe not exactly how I plan it to be, but close.

First there's what to wear. I have chosen a dress, black with blue print. Push-up bra, hold-up stockings, red boots and my only pair of fancy knickers. I hardly ever wear a dress, so a routine jacket with this outfit is unknown. I want him stood right outside the cinema door waiting. I want him to get hard the minute he sees me walking towards him. I want him to grab my hair and kiss me hard. I wonder if people looking at us will think I am too old for him. Unlikely, this is San Francisco. I have never been out with Jax in the daylight. He leaves for work before the sun comes up and we only meet after dark. Maybe he is a vampire and I am the young one out of us both.

I have just realised a flaw in my perfect fantasy. I can't buy the tickets first, if he arrives before me, and I don't want to buy the tickets in front of him. He is a man and may feel it emasculates him. That's likely crazy because he probably doesn't care.

Never mind, the rest of it still works.

In the cinema, I want to push up the armrest and nestle in his arms. I want him to not be able to stop kissing me. Then after the film I'll take him for a cocktail at the Marriott Hotel bar. It's a dark bar with views of San Francisco from every window. It looks like a film set from *Batman*. It is here that I want him to discover that I've removed my knickers and just gently explore me while still having a conversation. I would love to find a dark corner of the bar and have him fuck me, just a little bit, just enough to make me unable to walk straight because my pussy is so tender and full. I want him to stick his fingers in my mouth after he has played with me and then I can rinse off the taste of myself with red wine. I want to just look at him, talk crap and giggle. At some point, I want to teach him everything there is to know about pleasing a woman. Making him the most expert lover for me, and every other woman in his future. I want them to wonder who the woman was and send out a prayer of thanks to God for making him this good.

It's odd to be in a situation that you don't want to last forever. It would be the most selfish act if I did. I think it would break the spell if I could really be with him.

Tuesday 8th February

I've been on my own all day in the freezing flat trying to get some work done but I just kept having sex flashbacks instead of writing an article that could earn me some money. I had to stop writing twice to play with my new orange vagina-friendly vibrator, simply to buy myself some writing time. The problem was, once I got under the covers and pulled down my jeans to have a play, I didn't want to get out of bed again. It was warm! Then I would have a brilliant idea for the article and forget it by the time I was up and back in front of the computer. It's just felt like a waste of a day. I also hate days when I don't have clients, but I have been so focused on marketing the book that building the other part of my business has slipped.

By the time Anna came home I was desperate for conversation. I waited a while for her to put her bag down and start making her dinner before I pounced on her like a blocked dam that is suddenly released. I just love what Anna eats, so I like watching her cook and this was my excuse to hang in the kitchen!

Anna gets up at 6 a.m., goes running at the gym, comes back and has this green mush thing for breakfast, goes back to sleep for an hour then gets up and starts the day. She builds websites as well as being an actress. Basically she is one of those people I aspire to be, and fail at it. I've told Anna all about Jax. She thinks I am not connecting with my power and that's why I am attracted to a younger man. I have been known to intimidate people, when I do become powerful. But she told me that there is a difference between aggressive power and positive power. The problem with being connected to my positive power is that it attracts people. When you attract people they want something. People like basking in other people's energy and it's positive and light. But it's also lonely.

Anna said it's like being a big sweet pie that everyone just wants to get their fingers into. They pull out the cherries until nothing is left of the pie. When the pie has gone it's over. She says that our first responsibility is to ourselves. To live life in balance with what we give what we receive. You don't have to receive it from other people; you just need to now to replenish yourself with all of your cherries.

Anna is a good friend to have in the flat, although I try very hard not to act like a housewife with her in the role of returning husband. Working from home my whole world sometimes seems to be lived through the PC. Not only am I doing all of the work to push the book, I am also being my own PR person and expert marketer. Not to mention doing all of the social media and research for Green Café, and if I were to go out and get a bar job then I'd be contravening my visa. It all works out OK, but it does mean I am spending far too much time at home on my own. Even the dog gets bored of me. So I have to be careful when I do catch Anna in the kitchen for a coffee that I don't jump all over her like an excited Labrador puppy.

She has always lived in San Francisco, born and raised. But many of the friends she grew up with have become part of bridge-and-tunnel crowd or moved away completely because of the increase in rent. We have a good deal on the rent in this place. Anna is the master tenant, which means she manages the room rentals for the landlord and buys all the household stuff and splits the bill with us. She also keeps the kitchen spotless and has the best bedroom. I have learnt so much being in San Francisco about real green issues. We are so far behind in the UK. Anna cleans the flat with stuff like white vinegar and lemon juice. There is no bleach in the place at all and none of the products have anything nasty in them.

In the same way, Green Café has taught me so much about how saving water and light fittings can save businesses loads of money every year. As part of my job I have been setting up these events called 'Carrot Bombings', which is the opposite of a boycott. The idea is that when you have all of the right light bulbs and the right covers for the fridges or new water-saving flush systems in the toilets, then the coffee houses we serve save a fortune on their business bills. But it takes cash investment to buy all the right stuff in the first place, so many cafés are chasing their tails as they want to get green certified by the government with a nice green badge to display in their windows, but don't have the upfront ready money.

Believe it or not, there is a high level of competition between independent cafés, as coffee is a cult in its own right. Some coffee houses can have a queue going out of the door, while the chain brand next door might be empty. Here, the brand label on your cup says something about you. So if your favourite coffee shop also has a green certificate that also says something about you, and makes a difference to the coffee connoisseur's choice of café.

So a carrot bombing is when green cafés join with other environmental bodies, each with their own passionate social media followers. We then set a date with the café and all the profits that day go to greening-up their café towards the green certification. We then let all the greenies in San Francisco know, and they walk out of their way to go to that café on that day and will buy a little extra in the knowledge that they are buying coffee and cake for the planet! An orange carrot incentive to make the cafés green.

The first one I did of these was a café close to my home near Dolores Park. I advised them to have more products, yet still everything – and I mean everything – was gone by 3 p.m. It was as if a swarm of locusts had descended, leaving not even the crumbs of a flapjack behind them.

Often we are able to use the café house wars to our advantage. For example, if a coffee shop says they aren't interested in going green, we need only mention that we're working closely with their competitor to get a meeting with them. Then they ask questions about the other coffee house, and it's almost funny seeing them pretend not to be fishing for information.

On Valencia, two of them are at war. I heard a rumour that they used to be in business together but fell out over something, likely the difference between drip feed and espresso! What's interesting is that the dispute has divided the Mission community, as people are backing one or the other; and it comes down to whether you like the dark roast from one, or the rich roast from the other. This isn't just water-cooler conversation; this is cause for hot debate. You may even be shunned in the street for holding the wrong branded cup as you move closer to 20th Street down Valencia.

Being green is a way of life here, and very little in our flat goes to landfill, so if you don't want something anymore, you put a sign on it that says 'free' and before long someone takes it. I slept on a futon top that I found in the street when I first got here. In fact, my whole room is filled with things bought at garage sales, from thrift stores or found.

I remember being bullied and called 'Oxy' at school for wearing second-hand clothes, and yet, in the environmentally friendly capital of the Western world, I was ahead of my time. Still it's strange that in the rest of the world, the part without 3 per cent of the world's wealth that is, calling someone Oxfam would be quite a compliment I'd assume.

When I first moved here I used to chuck out plastic with the trash. Anna had to explain to me what the five bins in the laundry room where for. It even turned out that you weren't obliged to wash your empties because it is a waste of water. As long as it wasn't too soiled, and therefore wouldn't smell, the depot dealt with it.

What I've learnt from all this is that culture shock isn't always about people not laughing at your jokes. It's a whole level of life you have to adapt to. I can see why expats gravitate towards each other and talk about missing Jelly Babies, which are banned in the US, something to do with the yellow ones having something bad for you in them. That is other than sugar!

Me, I believe everyone should try living outside of their own culture. Just like every driver should try riding a pushbike or a motorbike. You only understand who you are by plonking yourself somewhere foreign. The only thing is, it changes you, and you only know that when you plonk yourself back where you came from and play spot the difference. Do that too many times and you become fragmented. Like a hard drive that looks like a game of Tetris, you have holes where people you love are missing, because they live somewhere else. You can call them over Skype and see their little faces squashed into small boxes and wave when you hang up the call. But who you are is made up of the unique blend of yourself and what is created in their company. When a person leaves your life, that unique blend goes with them. In the same way that a coffee bean has a taste that originates from its native soil – the rain that fell on the plant, the dog that peed on it (subject to taste), the sun that shone – and just the way it was roasted.

In fact coffee should really only be drunk in the country of origin. In hot countries you can have five shots of espresso throughout the day, and you don't get the coffee wobbles because you sweat it out. In those countries coffee allows you to work longer without needing a little nap in the afternoon, it is the pick-me-up for hot places. When you don't sweat coffee out of your system, because you live in Solihull, that's when five espressos will give you verbal diarrhoea and an anxiety complex.

I think if you take something or someone out of its real environment then you'll learn more about its nature. You can only understand yourself in relationship to something else, that's why we crave love and company. Not just love for another, but to truly learn who we are in reflection of someone else. The daft thing most of us keep looking for a soul mate – a mirror image – and, when we find them, we don't like what we see. That's why opposites attract.

Friday 11th February

The movie last night was really dull and I spent most of it just wishing the armrest wasn't there! Although I perked up when we got to the Marriott, and felt excited walking into the bar with Jax, and taking him up to the top floor to see the *Batman* film set. These kinds of posh hotels always give me a bit of a rush. I don't believe I belong in them. They are for people who have an excess of cash or people whose business pays for it. In fact, you have to have an excess of cash to even pay for a drink in this place and in a way that makes it exclusive and special. With a world outside of homeless people in the rain, I can think of better ways to spend money. But just so often, I like to think I am one of those people who have enough money to care about the world, make it a better place, and treat myself at the same time.

Still, I felt like I didn't fit in here. But not in the same way that I don't fit into Dolores Park, no one knows that I don't fit in there, which is what I like about it. Like being a foreigner in a country, you might look like everyone else, but you know you're not. Jax loved the bar, and immediately walked over to one of the windows before turning to me with a cheeky grin and saying, 'Brilliant' in a mock British accent to make me laugh.

He told me he loves how I like dark bars. It was

tempting to tell him all about how I had created this whole scene between us in my head. Of course I can't tell him that, this is one of the crazy things about women, we dream stuff up, wish it would happen then when it doesn't we feel disappointed even though we didn't tell anyone what we wanted. No one has ever asked me to marry them, I have never wanted to get married, but I know exactly how I would liked to be asked. But I couldn't possibly tell anyone, as the incentive has to come from them otherwise it doesn't count. To the right man who is listening, a woman drops a thousand clues.

Part of the bar was closed to table service, so everyone was squashed up together in one room. Still we managed to find a spot away from everyone in the part of the bar that was closed.

I went to the bathroom, slipped my knickers off and went to the bar. Then I realised I'd have to hold them while I looked for money in my purse. I hoped that the bartender wouldn't notice. But he totally did and threw me a look. Something crossed between concern for the general hygiene of the bar and curiosity. I walked back to Jax and totally fumbled dropping them in his lap while holding two glasses of red wine. In the darkness he didn't realise they were my knickers. When he did, he didn't know what to do with them, so he put them in his pocket like they were a hanky.

I remember working in a theatre as an usherette. I was secretly seeing the lighting guy who was called Andy and worked backstage. All the other usherettes had a crush on him, which of course made him all the more attractive. We would meet after work by the stage door. I had a key so we would sneak back into the theatre after closing. We had to crawl down the stairs to get past the alarm system sensors, and we couldn't put the lights on in case anyone saw them from outside and raised an alarm. I was still a virgin at the time so we only fooled around.

One night I got downstairs before him and ran though the sub-stage area and up the stairs onto the stage leaving a trail of wine red nylon uniform behind me. Emergency lights only lit the space and it was dark but when my eyes got accustomed to the light, I realised Andy was standing behind me clutching my discarded clothes. We started kissing and he dropped them to the floor, put his arms round my naked body and lifted me up so he was holding me off the floor. He was one of those people who are naturally strong, from doing a job where you have to lift stuff rather than going to the gym. There's something better about a natural build over a sculpted one. Effortlessly he lay me down on the stage floor opened my legs and started licking me. Not just focusing on my clit, but the whole of my pussy with big thick tongue brushstrokes like he was painting a set. I propped myself up onto my elbows to watch him, but I couldn't see much as the top of his head was in the way.

Leaning my head back, I looked into the auditorium of empty seats. Something about the vastness of the space was a turn on. Then I had the idea of this being the show and hundreds of eyes watching us. My sounds of pleasure were more dramatic that night, and echoed off the proscenium arch. He never did try to fuck me, he totally respected the fact I was a virgin, if he had even pushed it a little that night I would have given it up. It would have made quite a story, I could imagine telling people how I lost my virginity, on stage!

But he never did push it. I guess now, he only wanted something fun and didn't want the responsibility of taking my virginity. There is something amazing about the smell of a theatre, even after pantomime when the sticky sweet smell of children is still in the air. It was all very innocent. Afterwards we couldn't find my bra. He said he would come into the theatre early the next morning and find it before the cleaners arrived. He was sure that if anyone found it they would think an actress had dropped it during a quick costume change.

The next night, he pulled it out of his pocket, behind the confectionary counter where anyone could have walked passed and seen him. Of course I blushed and couldn't get the redness out of my cheeks for most of the evening and was totally aware that I was walking around with my bra tucked into the wine red blazer of my usherette uniform.

Jax and I watched the rain trickle down the window; and I realised that this wasn't going to be quite the sexy experience I'd been hoping for. As we talked, it was like sitting on the top of San Francisco but the table annoyed me as yet again there was an inanimate object between us – first the cinema armrest and then the stupid table. So, I moved to sit on his chair in-between his legs. We both faced out of the window and watched the rain. After we'd been chatting for a while, Jax said, 'You know, we're the same?'

'In what way?' I asked.

'You know the way you describe stuff and how it makes you feel?'

'Yeah?'

'I thought I was the only person who sees the world like that. It's like listening to myself think. I don't tell people half the shit I tell you. People tell me I'm really hard to get to know. But you like, know me.'

'I just know how to listen and I find you interesting.'

I realised then that our conversation is more meaningful to me than him running his hand up my leg to my pussy. But it worried me that I wanted that much talk and didn't care so much about the action. Feelings are dangerous things.

Jax seemed keen to continue the conversation too and said, 'Most people talk about stuff they want to do, things they have seen on TV, shit they wanna buy. You talk about real things. People, feelings and stuff. I get that, but no one else gets that. I don't have a girlfriend my own age as they wanna talk about shoes and shit. It's fucking dull. When we see a movie, you have stuff to say about it, things I didn't get see. You open the world up.'

'Really? No I'm just talking.' I said, dismissing his niceness.

'You do, I can't wait until you meet my friends.' He said grinning.

A cold chill went down my body! There is no way I can meet his friends. I really would feel my age.

We left the bar and on the way home Jax talked about his job. He told me that the coffee house is reviewing all the staff but his has gone well. It is really important for him to keep his job as the coffee shop is going to change location and he could get dropped from the new staffing system. It seems crazy to me to worry about losing a job that you have no intention of keeping. I know it is a matter of wanting to have control over your own destiny but I thought about how many times I have been sacked from a job. Every time it has been the best outcome, and since I've secretly wondered whether I did it to myself on purpose in order to get a universal kick up the backside to go and do what I really wanted to be doing – which was working in film. At twenty-one your time just seems too long, you laugh at people who tell you it flies by. It's not time that flies by, but your chances.

When we got home Jax showed me the hole in his trousers and told me that he needs to go clothes shopping! His hole revealed pants that could teach you how to make a paper airplane. Cute! I stripped my dress off and did my best to crawl up the bed wearing hold-ups and no pants. It was funny how I had been thinking about what I wanted to teach him. He was pretty much doing it without me needing to show him anything!

This morning he said he had woken up happy, which was unusual. Although, he still needed his coffee and cupcakes mantra to get out of bed. He got dressed in the dark again. As he got to the door, he turned round came back to the bed and kissed me in earnest. I melted. Even though I was kind of sure he knew what I wanted. I gave him $20, it was meant to be more but I wigged out on the fact that I was giving it to him after a night of sex.

Last night I told Jax of a possible job doing some deliveries for Green Café events and later that morning he sent me a text:

Great night. If I get another job, you won't have to pay for anything, but beer. Jx

I am stunned. We are suddenly shifting from being a paid thing to being a relationship thing. That, the kiss and the conversation make me realise how close I feel to him.

Now I am feeling panicked. I know I can't get this close to the boundary. It's in place for a reason. It's holding my feelings in a disposable container, and when the deal is done I know I will have to let go. One text message and the container has gone and I start to ache for him. Pulling myself together I write back saying that the job might be a one-off, and that I can't think of anything more fun to spend my money on. Who could argue with that?

A while later I send him a text asking him when he wants to meet to go shopping. No reply just yet. I think I will feel better if we do go shopping, then I will feel we are in business and not in love. I'm happy, very happy.

I've just received another visit from the UPS man, this time with a large box full of my books ready for me to send out to anyone who could let the world know of its existence. UPS man gave me his special smile, but somehow I have grown immune and I grinned back without the usual glint in my eye.

I am all set up with my introduction letter, press releases and Jiffy bags. I plan to send all these books to people who have expressed an interest from the PR launch. Although I'm not impressed with the PR Company I've hired and am disheartened at having to pay them *and* buy all the books to send out. I pay half price for the book, yet the likelihood is that I will spend more on getting this book out into the world than I will make on the book sales, which sucks. Of course, if it becomes a bestseller then it will be a different story.

I pause as I write out an address for a radio station in Seattle. I wonder if I will ever go to Seattle with Jax. I am now starting to get irritated with my own thinking. The book now is the important thing and yet I am horribly distracted from it. Perhaps it's an act of deliberate self-sabotage.

I had a conversation with my publisher last week and they expressed again the importance of raising my social media state further. Green Café have the same situation, they get more grants if they have a large social media following on Facebook and Twitter. It feels like narcissistic marketing, 'like me like my book', I'll give you free stuff and then you buy something. It's known as the 'jab jab punch' or 'giveaway, giveaway, sales pitch'.

I wanted to write a book to help people find love. Yet at the same time I love looking at some of my favourite authors posts, and I don't know if I like it more when they seem unreachable. It does feel unnatural to me, but if I want to be an author, these are the rules of engagement, and if I want another book published, my audience needs to tell me in 'likes'.

Saturday 12th February

I met Jax after he'd finished work in the Castro, the gay district of San Francisco. He had never been before and I loved the sheepish look on his face, as a guy checked him out as he walked up the street towards me. We went into a bookshop specialising in male porn. Lots of clichéd gay men were wearing leather caps and sporting beards. However, the purpose of us meeting in the Castro wasn't to titillate my enjoyment of the guys looking at my man – although it was fun, especially when the guy boys told me, 'Good luck, girl, he's cute!' – but to take him to the Levi's store and buy him some new jeans. I parked myself on the leather pouffe in the centre or the store and watched Jax survey the racks of jeans.

As is usual in the States, a sales guy was on him right away. Helping him to find the jeans he was looking for. He was taken off into the dressing room and then the server joined me, ready for our fashion show. Jax came out with the first pair on and the server fluttered around him, pulling them up high over his ass.

'Oh yes I love those,' he said.

Jax wasn't convinced and felt he needed a darker colour. After a few attempts it became clear that he was looking for ones that would fall off his ass, rather than show off his beautiful butt. Now my little fantasy of being

117

Richard Gere was crumbling, as I could feel my mothering self coming on. I took an intake of breath to convey that *hey, I'm wearing designer underwear, falling-down jeans just come out of prison look sucks,* then thought better of it. Well I guess it might be nice to see the crack of his ass over his pants! By the time we left, he had new underwear, jeans and a grey T-shirt, which felt so soft to the touch that I couldn't wait to feel his chest through it. He looked so pleased. Afterwards, we stopped for coffee and a cupcake, and I slid a copy of my book across the table to him.

'This is *your* book! Look it has your name on it! That's super cool you must be psyched,' he said. Then a wave of sadness came into his eyes, 'I would love to have an achievement like this, my own script in my hands.'

'You very much might and more, even red-carpet stuff. I had done nothing at your age, so don't give yourself a hard time!'

He didn't look at me, as if what I was saying was an impossible fantasy.

'So are you up for something crazy?' I asked him.

'Sure why not?' He replied.

I took a deep breath, and paused for a spilt second wondering if this was just another ruse to spend time with him or if I really wanted to do this. I must have been looking at the table because when I looked up, he was grinning and looking excited.

'Well you know I told you about the sex club and the Pink Party? I have been asked to speak there, and well it's on Monday night. Will you come as my protector?' I asked.

'I'm in, set it up, that's the dopest fuckin' shit in the world,' he said excitedly.

I made an arrangement to meet up with him. He asked me what he should wear but I didn't think it really mattered. We said goodbye and I sent him off on the tram back to his place in the Tenderloin. I wanted to take him back to my place, of course, but he said he had a meeting with his cousin. As the tram pulled away, he gave me a grin out of the window and pushed the book up against the glass, and I became aware that one day that would be the last time I saw that face. I do this with every amazing connection, I start to feel sad about its inevitable end even when its not ended. I do it over my dog, everything. It's like I have to prepare for the loss in advance, so the loss isn't as hard. I know it's such bullshit. I started to think about my future and what I wanted and really at what point I needed to make a move. The inevitability that everything ends somehow makes everything more special.

Monday 14th February

Mission Street was decked out in love hearts and pink ribbons for St Valentine's Day. A golf cart giving away mini cupcakes nearly hit me when I looked the wrong way when crossing the street. The three people aboard the cart thought it was the funniest thing ever and gave me a cupcake. I asked for a second one for my boyfriend, the words tripping out of my mouth as if it was no word of a lie. But the word lover would have been more appropriate, I feel too old to have a boyfriend, and man friend is ridiculous.

The cupcake was a red velvet one with red sponge and white frosting, and designed to be unwrapped and put into your mouth whole. The frosting melted on my tongue, while I crushed the sponge against the roof of my mouth into a rich gooey mess.

Jax was early and waiting for me on Mission Street, and I spotted him looking at a display row of jeans. They were on mannequins that were only made from the hips down – a long row of long legs and giant peach bottoms. I distracted him from the perfect backsides of the mannequins with the cupcake. Then went on to tell him that I'd have to stuff a whole box of man-sized tissues into the back of my kickers to fill those jeans.

I was always curious as a child as to why they were

called 'man-sized tissues', as if a man produces more snot than a woman. Surely it would depend on the size of the cold. Could you measure a cold in snot? Then, when I became an adult, it dawned on me that perhaps the marketing analogy was a sexual one – man-sized tissues for soaking up sperm.

Of course, I thought it totally appropriate to tell Jax my revelation about man-sized tissues, and when he looked at me like a dog being shown a card trick, I realised that I must be freaking out. I always talk complete shite when I am nervous.

I remember teaching my first yoga class: my breathing was all over the place and I just kept talking and talking about all the crazy names for the poses. I had taught English for years to classes of foreign students, but only realised I was scared of public speaking when I had to get a class to focus on their breathing and couldn't get mine under control. Where we are going tonight isn't just public speaking about my book, its potentially public sex.

Jax and I walked a while; I was pulling my wheeled case full of books. These wheelies are not made for short people. They drag out longer behind you when you're short, so there is more chance of someone falling over them. In London I'd bend my elbow to hold the case closer to my body and make it less of a trip hazard but there's so much room on US pavements that I could add a sidecar to it. Make it a four-wheeler. Jax asked me if I wanted him to carry it, and I said no because it was heavy. Although, it's interesting how men don't like pulling these things, they can only lift them, so Jax left it to me until we reached the steps of the club.

The club manager I'd met at Wicked Grounds greeted

us and then proudly showed us round the club. It was beautifully decked out and romantically lit but the number of beds was daunting. I set up my books on a table ready to sell them and after a while the audience for the evening started to enter. Jax sat to my right but well out of the way. I was given a short introduction to a room of about fifteen people. It was a really small gathering, but an eclectic bunch all dressed up, some in fantasy costume and some not. I was in a bright red dress with a push-up bra, which I'd accompanied with stunning red lipstick.

During the presentation, I tried to focus on the parts of the book that would be interesting to them. There was a section on spirituality and kink, so I discussed that; and a bit on role-play and male-female dynamics, which I thought they might like. I had discovered that many Americans considered Monica Lewinsky, crawling on her hands and knees after the former President Bill Clinton's dick, to be an act of kink because it wasn't done in the bedroom. Personally, I see it more as an act of desperation – I mean, have you seen that man's jaw! Knowing not to talk politics, I avoided that subject!

Arriving late came a short lady in a corset and hat who sat down in the front row, her corset lifting higher as she did, so that any evidence of her having a neck disappeared behind her large breasts. She made me think of how a bulldog might look pushed into a polo neck jumper, as her chins had also been pushed up to her jawline.

Halfway through my talk, she started firing questions at me and, when she spoke, I couldn't help but notice that her voice sounded restricted, as though her windpipe was being compressed – which was highly likely given the size of her bosom. Her first couple of questions were fairly innocuous but then they started to become more and more personal. Answering her questions about my sex life, I started to worry whether Jax was feeling uncomfortable about what question might come out of her talking mound of breasts next.

I also think she assumed that the British are reserved. But the big cultural difference between the Americans and the British, from what I have seen, is that the Californians are all doing it and the British are all talking about it. But she seemed set on embarrassing me.

'I have another question.'

'Sure ask away.'

'As a sex-guide author, do you use your book as a mandate for all your partners and will you in the future?'

'No,' I replied, 'I choose lovers with imaginations and trust they can teach me for my next book.'

'Who did you write the book for?'

'Many of my clients are women who have gone too far into their masculine side. The women's liberation movement was a movement towards masculine rather than feminine power. There is now social discord, as some women are either emasculating their partners or only attracting weak men. The book is about using sex as a way to rectify the balance because, over time, when two people become partners they lose the sexual dynamic between the masculine and feminine. This is happening faster than at any other time in our relationships.'

'Does this mean you're not bisexual, you have only written about heterosexual sex?'

I fixed her with a look and in my very best clipped British accent said, 'It sounds to me like you are interviewing me for a job, are you intending to put an offer on the table or is this a personal enquiry for a *particular position?*'

I said that final phrase in such a way that it would have made Frankfurter in *Rocky Horror* proud. And with that, I won over the crowd, a few whoops and I was in with the most amazing array of interesting-looking people. The woman's face fell. Even her breasts looked like they had deflated and she said nothing more to me. The room became electric and I was on a roll. After the talk, people bought books and wanted them signed and then bought me drinks. I was on such a high that I almost forgot Jax was there. He watched me and kept close, some people talked to him but he made it clear he was with me.

One woman gestured towards Jax and asked me, 'Where did you get your puppy? He's adorable.'

It was turning out to be perfect and nothing I needed to fear. However, I still had my nervous drinking head on, which meant I was drinking far more than I meant to. The main party had started and I was still in the building, and now there was no way I was leaving until I had seen those rooms – this time with people in them. Jax and I packed up the unsold books and put the wheelie in the cloakroom. I checked with Jax but he said he was OK and up for having a look around too.

The main room, with the largest bed, seemed to be alive with bodies. We couldn't really see anything in the half-light, but we could hear gasps and groans. Jax kept saying, 'Oh My God' and, as we became more accustomed to the light, we could see more and more. Then suddenly, I started to I feel like a pervert for watching something I wasn't meant to see, and I didn't let my eyes stay long in any one area, just in case someone caught me looking.

I noticed a couple next to a lamp, and the woman

seemed to be looking at me while her man's head was between her legs. I could tell she wanted me to watch, and then I felt it was totally fine to watch and, in fact, some people were there to be watched!

We reached one room and when we slowly pushed open the door, there was a man in the centre of the room attaching a blue electric charger to the nipples of three women that were standing round him. They jumped and giggled when he did it. We closed the door again, and tried not to let the people in the room hear our nervous laughs.

Jax said, 'Fake tits!' with regards to the girls, and I think he was right because they didn't look like real boobs, but it felt weird to be commenting on their breasts when there was a man with a blue lightening rod electrifying them! It fact it's weird where your mind doesn't go in situations like these.

In a room called the hospital the walls were covered in plastic sheeting, which glistened in the white light. In one corner there was a white see-through vanity screen and lights behind it meant you could see everything going on, on the other side. It looked like a girl was on a table with her legs apart having a smear test with one person at her head and another between her legs. By the way their shadows were moving it looked like she was being fucked with some implement like a dildo. I was transfixed.

Jax broke my gaze to show me a man in a glass coffin. As I looked more closely, it was an adult-sized incubator with a man inside. People had their hands in the rubber glove-lined holes running down the side of the Perspex box. They stroked his body, pinched him, but kept their touch away from his fully erect cock.

Another man was perched on the edge of a bar stool

while a woman sucked his cock. She had a collar and lead around her neck, which the man was holding and seemed to be using to control her speed. Her mouth slowly moved down the shaft gracefully, right up towards the base. You could tell this was all about his control over her and pleasure rather than about making him cum. Every so often, she looked up at him lovingly and he would touch her face or hair.

Near by was a girl in a nurse's uniform bent over an office table and being spanked by a doctor in a white lab coat, complete with a stethoscope around his neck and facemask.

Rather than being shocked by any of this, I was intrigued. It felt more like an acting performance than anything truly about sex. Walking out of the room by a different door, we found a cage, with men on the floor being stood on by women. The women were barefoot and supporting some of their body weight by hanging onto the bars of the cage. The bulldog woman from the talk was in there too, standing almost on the face of a man and having her toes sucked.

I wanted to be involved in the carnival of kink, and was repelled by it at the same time. I wasn't sure I had the balls to do it. I could already feel myself be a bit too drunk to be able to think clearly. So Jax suggested getting a drink, I immediately replied, 'Why not?' But I knew very well why not, but I wanted the drink as an excuse to do what I know I wanted to do and I knew very well it would have nothing to do with the drink.

We headed to the bar and sat on stools talking to the bartender. Behind us was a girl who looked like she had just fallen off the set of *Little House on the Prairie*.

She had ringlets like Nellie Oleson and was wearing a cream bridesmaid dress. I found her fascinating; she was just sitting there on her own. I felt a predatory feeling come over me, like a lion that's just spotted a wounded deer. It frightened me slightly and I couldn't help thinking, *If she's giving ME (nice, spiritual, kind and lovely) that reaction, I better make sure she is all right.* Like the moment you see a woman's purse could be lifted out of her handbag. You tell her to close her handbag because someone could take her purse, but the point is, you thought of it first!

I decided to go and talk to her to make sure she was OK, but as I sat next to her I realised that this was a come-on, and obviously a welcome one.

'I can't touch you,' she said, 'because my hands are tied up behind my back.'

I bit my lip at that horribly inviting comment. 'I'm not going to hurt you,' I tell her. I have never understood why men take advantage of women, and then suddenly I got it, and wondered if this is what it feels like to be a man with a woman in unwalkable heels and a tight skirt. I'm not talking about rape, as rape is an act of war against women, I'm talking about seduction. *Dangerous liaisons*, pure and simple. I could feel Jax eyes burning into us as we sat on the sofa, and the idea of putting on a show for him drove me even more. I lifted her dress to put my hand underneath the layers and layers of taffeta until my hand landed on the nylon resting on the inside of her thigh. She made a small gasp and pushed her hips up towards me, to encourage my hand to move further up her leg. Pressing my lips to hers, soft, warm and slightly wet, she kissed me back. Taking more control I ran my hand up her leg until I could feel the lace at the top of her stocking. I paused to finger its texture and started to kiss her hard, pushing my tongue into her mouth only to have to greeted by hers, I heard a faint noise behind me and knew it was Jax adjusting his view on the bar stool.

I loved the fact he was watching, as I moved up to run my middle finger over her pussy and found that she was wet right through the silk of her pants. I pulled back from kissing her to watch her face, as I pulled her knickers open at the side and massaged her clitoris. Her eyes and head rolled back, her mouth dropped open and I knew all I wanted to do was watch her cum. I brought my mouth close to the side of her face, and asked her, 'Do you like that?'

'Yeah.'

'Do you want me to make you cum?'

'Yes.'

'You're such a good girl, are you going to do everything I say?'

'Yes,' she gasped.

'Well then I might let you cum, but then again, I might just play with your clit a while longer seen as you can't stop my fingers exploring anywhere they like.'

I took both hands and pulled her knickers down and she lifted her ass a little to aid me. They dropped wet down by her ankles. I told her to open her legs wide, and I resumed massaging her clit while ensuring that her dress covered her womanly parts. The dress was strapless so it was easy to pull it down to reveal her breasts, and I went from one nipple to the other flicking and sucking with my mouth. She had one of those perfumes that was slightly too sweet, perhaps something that Britney Spears' might endorse as her scent. Even over the top of the perfume,

I could smell her pungent wetness and her arousal building. I glanced up to look at Jax, but an audience of people now obscured him. Having an audience wasn't daunting, I loved it, and it made me want to perform and use her body as a puppet. Pushing my finger into her pussy I made her gasp, I used my thumb to run rings around her clit until I was found it hard to move my middle finger inside of her as her orgasm built and her pussy got tighter. Her hips were now swaying upwards against my hand, as her orgasm seemed to take control of her whole body movement apart from her hands, which were still tied behind her back.

I moved my mouth close to her ear again, 'You're a dirty little slut, what are you?'

'A dirty slut,' she breathed.

The word 'slut' doesn't sound the same in an American accent. You really have to pronounce the final 't' to make it work.

I flicked her nipples again with my tongue and gave them a little nip with the tips of my teeth. I knew I was bang on target with my thumb on her clit, so I took some of the pressure off to prolong her orgasm and build the sensitivity. Her hips pushed upwards, but I pulled my hand a little back, so she couldn't impale herself on my fingers any more deeply than her G-spot.

'You're such a pretty girl, do you deserve to cum?'

'Yes.'

'Have you been good?'

'I'll be good to you,' she said in a pleading groan and I quickened my massage.

'Like feeling my fingers in your pussy, slut?'

By now she was getting so close to climax, out of words and just making these really sweet pleading, breathy cries of bliss. With my mouth so close to her ear, I found myself saying things that even I found unbelievably shocking.

'Yes baby, cum you little slut, squirt your juice on my fingers, yes cum on cum.'

With one loud cry she came, her breasts rising and falling with gasps for air. I covered her mouth with mine and kissed her hard and frantically, I then pushed my wet fingers into her mouth and I made her lick my fingers clean. Her man, the one who had tied her up, came over and introduced himself to me.

'Nice performance,' he said.

I turned to find Jax standing right next to me. He leaned into my ear and said, 'I am going to fuck you so hard when we get home.'

I went to the bathroom and looked at myself in the mirror as I washed my hands. I don't know if I expected to see somebody different. An empowered woman, fearless predator but I just saw me, with slightly mushed eyeliner in the corner of my eyes. I corrected that and stepped out to find protector Jax right outside the door. In fact, he wasn't protecting me, he was spooked. The moment I'd left him, he had been approached by a number of people and now was feeling the urgent need to leave!

We said thank you to our host, grabbed the wheelie and headed out onto Mission Street. There were often a lot of homeless people in this area that hung out at the BART stations of 24th and 16th streets. One side of Mission Street was considered to be safe and the other side, the one getting closer to Van Ness Avenue, was not. But it all looked the same to me, and I was told many of the homeless were actually ex US military.

As we walked up the street Jax started approaching

people and saying things like, 'Good evening', 'How you doing' or 'Nice to see you'. Sometimes it sounded as if he had a silly British accent and sometimes like he was on drugs. I laughed at first, but then he started really getting in people's way. He was doing it to everybody – homeless people, couples, women on their own. I tried to pull him back over towards me and engage with him. But he wrapped his arm around my head rather than my shoulder and started saying, 'You are BRILLIANT, you are, most brilliant' in a British accent.

I tried to be funny back, but I couldn't quite match his energy and was pleased when we got back to the flat. Luckily my roommates were out because he wasn't being quiet when we got in. We sat outside on the fire escape stairs, while the dog took a pee. He rolled a spliff, which was the first time I had ever seen him do that. He had never smoked pot in my company but then I have never made a girl cum in his, so I decided not to make a big deal of it.

'You know what's wrong with the world?' he asked me.

'Where shall I start?' I quipped back.

'Fear!' He said. 'Most people are too shit scared to do anything with their lives, too shit fucking scared to make a decision...even. Fuckin' pussies!'

He was now starting to trouble me. I started to wonder if I had taken this too far and he was angry with me.

'You're not like that, you're better than everyone else,' he said. 'You take the world by the horns, you do shit with your life, and you're not scared.'

'They say there are only two fears in life, losing what

you have and not getting what you want.' I said, hoping he'd started to calm down soon.

'Bullshit, what about hurting those you love and letting those you love down.'

'OK so four fears…' I said, but I didn't get to finish because he grabbed me hard by the hair and kissed me. I still felt a little afraid of him; I had never seen him like this. I didn't think he was drunk. He smoked quickly, offered me some, but I shook my head.

In the bedroom he ripped my clothes off and I had to grab the condom otherwise he wouldn't have bothered. I don't know where he was, but he wasn't with me in the room. My mind was racing and I didn't feeling connected to him at all. Right after he had cum, he pulled the condom off, chucked it on the floor and fell asleep.

Lying next to him I felt completely alone. I wanted to cry, but I didn't know if I could control the sobs enough not to wake him up. I'd been so clever, inspirational and foolhardy. I'd acted like the woman I want to be, and yet I am so far away from who she is, that the act of her makes me miss her more and makes me feel so horribly lonely.

Sex clubs and young boys, what the hell was I thinking?

I believe I am much more emotionally resilient than I really am, and sometimes my misperception of myself catches up with me. Like a complicated grief disorder when you're dad dies, you don't cry and then six month later you lose it because next door's cat gets run over. What was I thinking coming to the States? How did I ever think a new life would be what I needed? Wherever you go, there you are. I didn't need a new life I needed a new me. I was doing everything external to find it and nothing internal.

Slow, hot tears fell down my cheeks, my throat hurt from trying to hold back the cries and sniffles. I closed my eyes and let sleep take me to somewhere better than how I was feeling in that moment. The morning would be better. In the morning Jax would get out of bed with his 'cupcakes and coffee' mantra and tuck the duvet in around me to stop to cold air touching my skin. In the morning, I would be OK with this again.

Of course in the morning it's never quite the same. I pretended to be asleep while Jax got ready to leave thinking I would text him later and find out the lay of the land.

Friday 18th February

Nat and I went for Bi-Rite ice cream. Her favourite flavour is called 'secret breakfast' and it's made from cornflakes and bourbon. I told her all about what had happened with Jax, but hesitated about confessing the possible cause – my fumble with Nellie Oleson. She clocked it, however, as that woman never misses a trick! So I told her the whole thing. She wasn't at all shocked.

'HELLO! This is San Francisco! Most guys would kill for a night like that, are you kidding me?'

I haven't heard from Jax since and I have decided not to contact him. Nat thinks I am doing the right thing. We went for a bit of a drive and took my dog for a walk along the beach. Just being by the ocean made me forget about the whole thing and I started to feel less like I had just broken a puppy. As we made our way back to the car kicking off the sand as we did, I heard my phone ping and it was a message from Jax.

Hey Sam, I have some cupcakes from work going to waste, would you like me to stop by and give them to you? Jx

Nat thinks that's an apology! I let him know I wasn't at home, but would love the cupcakes. By the time Nat pulled up in the car there was a box by the door, which somehow he'd managed to leave behind the locked gate. I text him to say thank you and asked him how he'd managed his Houdini trick with the cupcakes. He texted back that he stopped the UPS man delivering a package to my landlord and gave it to him. Apparently the UPS man called me, 'that cute girl with the books'.

Nat decided to stay for a coffee and help me with the cupcakes. A day of ice cream and cupcakes is totally fine if you've had a long walk on the beach! I felt relieved that everything must now be fine with Jax even though I haven't seen him. We made a date by text to go to the cinema again.

Even now, we still don't call each other. I don't try any more and not because I think he might be sleeping or with friends. I'd just hate to call and hear him have a 'just some girl' attitude in front of his friends. Nat decided to hangout and we went over to the DVD rental and got a documentary called *The Bridge*. We don't have a TV, just a big screen and projector that we set up in the living room, so I mostly watch catch-up or films.

I love the DVD place because they carry the most interesting stuff, are really helpful and always have a treat for the dog. Sometimes when we walk past, the dog pulls for a treat and I end up hiring a film, as the dog is so insistent about going in. She also gets lots of fuss from the staff.

The Bridge was about the people who have jumped off the Golden Gate Bridge. They set up cameras on the bridge to catch the footage of the jumpers and then interviewed their living relatives. It was a fascinating film, and part of its point was to question why the state of California hasn't put up a net to catch the jumpers – the authorities think it will ruin the look of the bridge. People travel from all over the US to jump because death is almost certain. Except there was this one guy on the documentary that changed his mind, halfway down, curled into a ball but broke every bone in his body. He would have drowned but was saved by a sea lion that kept his head above the water until the coastguard picked him up. Apart from the sea lion bit, it wasn't a rom com but it made Nat cry but then she's very empathic.

I was confused and wondered whether there were two guys eating chips and placing bets on who would jump, while going through the film rushes. It was powerful and moving. Nat and I shared our suicide method of choice and then had that 'No, but I would never do it, thought about it, yes, do it, no, no!' conversation.

I went to bed thinking, people come to San Francisco to get a new life, visit a prison or die. Interesting place!

Monday 21st February

I didn't have an umbrella and the rain came down like it was kissing my face. I floated over puddles. I was the only one smiling and not rushing. Under the shelter of the extended ceiling at the Metreon cinema, I stood and watched the rain falling in slow motion. You wouldn't know that the droplets were there if you didn't see the lights bouncing off them.

The rain became heavier and with that a sense of urgency filled the air. I watched the people running. Felt I had vanished. Like the time I took shelter from the rain under the stoop in a church in New Orleans. I felt like I was one of the vampires, you couldn't see me, you couldn't smell me, I was dead yet not dead. Police cars chased down the street with sirens blaring. At one point they came down two connecting streets and nearly hit each other. I remembered where I was, an English girl about to meet an American boy on a date at the cinema in California. How many films have I watched with that backdrop? John Cusack about to step out the phone booth, it always seems to rain in John Cusack films. Everything felt like an American movie playing in slow motion.

I thought about the journey I'd taken to get here. Selling my house, giving away my things, the last yoga class and the gift my students gave me, all on a dream that feels so different now this is my life. But it's not my life. I cannot fall in love with it, if a date on a visa says I can't keep it. Its inevitable end makes it all the more beautiful. And I must remember to live in the moment because one day this will be a memory. I hope I don't look back and think that this is the greatest part of my life because I've noticed that with getting older. You start to wonder when that memory will be. You hope that the future is getting better; in the past it always was. I am now at an age when you are supposed to give up that hope and settle down. Let your life becomes about something greater than yourself like having a child. But in this moment, I am any age. I'm just a girl meeting a boy on a date to the cinema. It's really cold; I remember why I don't wear dresses.

Now where the hell is he? A text from him tells me that he's running late. Via a text conversation, we establish that he'll be here as the film starts, what popcorn he wants and that he wants me to get him some sweets I've never heard of, called Sour Patch Kids. I have had a Jelly Babies craving since I arrived in the States, so am hoping they taste similar.

I get what he wants and wait for him on the fifth floor with the tickets. To stop the rising anxiety, I play an arcade game and shoot some *Jurassic Park* dinosaurs. I figure that holding a gun in this dress and boots looks sexy, some kind of phallic image. Then he arrives, walking up next to me, he says hello and then kind of grabs me and gives me a hug. We talk non-stop as we walk down the long corridor to screen fifteen, laughing and chatting about the Pink Party. Fifteen is about the age I feel. We find a seat and Jax is as bummed as I am that the armrest won't go up.

The Sour Patch Kids weren't a patch on Jelly Babies! The popcorn doesn't even get touched – it sits on the floor because we were too busy being in each other's arms to be bothered to move and pick it up. Personally I was too busy feeling intoxicated by Jax's smell. At times during the film, apart from laughing at how bad it is, I just closed my eyes and felt his company – his big hands caressing my inner thighs. Despite what happened the other night, I felt safe. In fact, it is the first time that I've felt safe since being in America. In fact the first time I have felt safe in a long time. It's not as if I needed to trust Jax to do anything if something happened. Like if there was an earthquake and he would carry me out of a burning building like Nicholas Cage. It is the whole place and situation. I remember thinking, *I don't have to do anything, I'm in the dark, I am held, all I have to do for the next two hours is stay here, like this, and that is perfectly OK. Nobody expects anything else of me, just for this time.*

Of course time moves and now I am dizzy with the exhilaration of the film and the trance state I was in throughout it. It is still raining when we leave the cinema and Jax is proud that he has found an umbrella in the street earlier and it works perfectly.

And then the spell breaks when Jax puts it up and doesn't put it over my head, just his own. As the rain splashes my face like a cold-water wake-up slap, I am filled with sadness, nothing has changed since the last time we saw each other.

Umbrellas were a turning point in my long-term relationship with Simon too – the ex I'd bought the house with in London. Coming from a family who didn't have much money as I grew up, small things were a symbol of

139

wealth for me. Black umbrellas with leather bent handles were one of those symbols. There was something so typically upper class about the long black umbrella with the pointed end and the curved handle. It went along with the bowler hat and the pinstriped suit. I got a John Lewis gift voucher when I left my English teaching job, and I bought two umbrellas: one for a man and one for a woman. I loved holding them. I didn't even take them out of the house as I used a small handbag-sized one when it was raining. Then one day, Simon went to take the man's one out. I asked him to look after it, as he was good at losing things. I told him that I really liked them and they had meaning for me. He scoffed at me and promptly left it on the train. I was devastated but couldn't tell him because I thought he would think I was stupid. What it meant to me was that he really didn't love me. If he loved me he would have taken care of something that meant something to me. He lost my first edition hardback of Anne Rice's *The Vampire Lestat* the same way. I had asked him not to take it out of the house, and he left it on the train.

I could list so many things, and each one became a pebble that I put in a bag labelled 'wrong'. When the bag became heavy enough I dumped him with the bag. The truth is I wish I could have communicated to him what all these incidents added up meant to me. I guess for him they added up to the things meaning more to me than him. He was an only child from an affluent background. Items are not replaceable when you have four siblings. I grew up in second-hand clothes and learning to take care of everything. I know there is a link between self-esteem and stuff. I wonder where we would be if we'd had an authentic venerable conversation. I just didn't know how to do it, because when he scoffed at the small requests how could I open my heart? Here I am now with Jax in the rain, and again I would rather get wet than tell him that I feel hurt. A drip from the corner spike of the umbrella hits my eye. I wipe it away before my mascara runs. The water no longer feels like kisses, it feels like tears.

He doesn't know how I am feeling. We reach BART Station on Market Street; it's the place where our paths home diverge or converge, the point where he could come home with me. I tell him I'm exhausted and ask him if it's OK to call it a night. He puts the umbrella over me, plants a kiss on my lips and with a 'Catch you later' walks away before I can even take a step down the stairs.

When I reach the last step, I start to laugh. A woman singing, *Cry Me a River* is echoing through the subway, and this immense feeling that everything has a meaning swallows me up. Nothing is by accident and that the universe has a sense of humour.

Tuesday 1st March

I've just received a text from Jax:

> Just got fired from a D-list celebrity's pet cupcake
> shop. I really don't know if I can get over this one...
> And thus I sip Cerveza Pacifico at an Internet café
> waiting for my cousin. Just thought you'd want to
> know. It's a whole new ball game from here for me.

My inner rescuer archetype voice in my head pops up
with, *Yay, we can give him a loan (that way he'll be tied to
me).* Followed by, *Let him move into your room (that way
he'll be dependent on me).* Luckily I know this voice is the
voice of manipulative relationship insurance and it is ugly!
Help is often the sunny side of control. So I stop making
his whole drama my drama, and I send him a lovely text
telling him that I hope his cousin comes up with some
great ideas for him. Well, one much better than paying me
for sex, which was his last brain wave.

I decide it's time to pull myself together and switch
focus. It's all likely to get messy from here and the best
thing I can do, is let him go. I grab the dog and we go for
a walk round Dolores Park, pick up some ice cream from
Bi-Rite and get a film for the evening.

By the time I get back Anna is making coffee in the

kitchen. She also believes that everything has a meaning, and even when something bad happens you can perceive it as such. We both might be making it up, but the idea makes us happy and most of life is about making up what everything means anyway, so why not give it a positive meaning. Anna and I make a popcorn date to watch the film later that evening.

I had to wait for her to get ready so we started watching the film later than I normally would. That meant I was still getting ready for bed when the phone rang at 11 p.m. No one rings me that late. Jax's never calls me and it wasn't his number but still I picked up in anticipation that it was him.

'Hey Sam!'

'Hi,' I reply but I don't recognise the voice.

'Do you know who this is?'

I pause, and then a face pops into my mind, 'Dean?'

'Wow you remembered me, the guy who didn't call you right? I am so sorry about that. I'd just broken up with a girlfriend when I met you, and then she came back on the scene, so I couldn't call you and then that didn't work out and so I was wondering if we could hook up?'

Now, at this point, I am in a state of shock, however, also very happy to get an ego boost at this moment in time. Gratified by the fact that he didn't call for noble reasons fluffs my ego self into a state of instant un-jilted happiness.

'Sure why not,' I say, keeping it casual.

'OK great, I have a new job, and get off work at 1 a.m., I'll stop by your place tonight, see you then, byeeeee.'

The phone goes dead and somehow I have set up a booty call and not a date. How the hell did that happen?

I don't know that much about Dean, we didn't talk

a lot the last time. I know he is about the same age as me. He is mixed race and has a strong identity around that. He doesn't like being called black, and had a whole rant to me about the fact people call Obama black.

'He is not America's first black president, he's America's first mixed-race president,' he said while making me a cocktail.

On top of this, Dean isn't much taller than me, so that's a potential whole load of issues as I am vertically challenged myself. This line of thinking is typical of me. Before he has even come over I am working out what will be the catalyst for us breaking up. This being the case, it might be much simpler if he just comes over for sex, as it will save me a whole load of analysing.

I have gay friends who have had a person just come over to the house to have sex. I guess there is nothing wrong with it as such. I could stop it by calling him back. But I don't, instead I go to bed and get woken up by a text saying he's outside and doesn't know what bell the flat is.

We start kissing without much conversation and I don't try to offer coffee this time. I make some joke of saying 'Now where were we last time.' It starts out as a faked sexual connection until Dean then decides he is into it and takes control of the situation. His body is very lean, so there is definition of his pecks though his shirt, which seems just a bit too tight. In fact everything about him is tight, his butt cheeks, arms, tummy. He made a comment last time about the definition of my yoga arms, so he clearly works out, but isn't one of those big guys. More a Bruce Lee than a Vin Diesel and clearly is a seasoned professional when it comes to women. He sets about me, multitasking my body with fingers, tongue, legs and arms.

He knows what he wants and he wants all of it at once. I put the condom on him as he was ready to enter me without it, and that wasn't going to happen.

He starts fucking me from behind, in one of those porn-regimented ways, and keeps saying, 'Do you like that baby?'

Awkward as I could hardly say, 'No actually your penis is a bit spiky and it's smacking on my cervix.' So instead, I reposition my hips and say in my best porn voice, 'Ooh yeah like that.'

I knew I wasn't into it, I personally find it hard to go from one guy to another. It feels to me that when you make love a person gets absorbed into you. Almost as if there is a residual of that person's aura still connected to you. I have always put it down to a different smell, or different pheromones, on my skin from two men don't blend, even after several showers.

Whilst researching for the book, I discovered that on an MRI scan a woman's brain lights up after orgasm and in a man's brain the lights go off. Scientists believe this is so a woman can leave her partner asleep after sex and go off and find another mate who may have more baby-viable sperm. That's why one-in-five children in a family actually have a different father. For me, despite all this experimentation, I'm really a one-girl guy and I'm really feeling that right now...in the middle of having sex with someone else. I am faking even being present in the room, as my whole being is somewhere else, in another room with someone else.

He reaches over and rubs my clit and asks again, 'You like that?'

'Yes that's doing nicely thank you!'

I start to think about the things I said to my Nellie Oleson lookalike in the kink club and start to wonder if I had been as hot as I thought I was, by saying that stuff. I know saying it had turned me on and it seemed to be the thing that made her cum hard over my fingers. Thinking about her was making me feel more in the moment with Dean.

He massages my breasts and makes approving comments about how firm they are, another befit of yoga. Every so often he gives my ass a hard slap and then drops spit on it. I'm hoping he's not thinking of trying to push his dick in there! There is something about being used as a sex object. You have a choice, enjoy it for what it is, which is fucking, or feel robbed of an event that should have involved you. I decide to make it my own fantasy around what was happening so it didn't feel abusive. Not so much him being abusive towards me, but me towards myself. Something about being given permission to be selfish about my own pleasure meant I don't have to consider how close he is to cumming or anything he needs. Being clever or smart in bed I make it all about me and within moments of doing so, I come very hard.

Dean likes head, giving it and getting it, so soon after I have cum he pulls off the condom and thrusts his dick into my mouth. Blow jobs are an art form and impossible to do well when someone is fucking your mouth so hard the best you can do is cover your teeth by inverting your lips around them. He grabs my hair to hold my head still and thrusts so fast I can feel indentations being made by my teeth into my gums. He keeps trying to finger my pussy, which is more uncomfortable than pleasurable. Two solid fingers poking away at your entrance defies the shape of a woman, it always makes me want to yell, 'THERE IS A U-BEND!'

No matter how I move away from his fingers to make him stop, he follows me around the bed with them. It boggles my mind that some people can't feel when you don't want something. Finally I make him cum using hands and mouth, but it seems to take an eye-watering, jaw-aching long time.

Afterwards we sat on the bed a while and talked. It seemed that everything I said he disagreed with. Even when I was talking about how I felt about something, he told me I was wrong to feel like that. It was an arm wrestle in smartness and after everything he said he said, 'You hear what I'm sayin'? You understand me? You know what I mean?'

Fuck me you're not talking to a total idiot.

He lives in Oakland and he made it sound like a ghetto, like parts of South London but with more gun than knife crime. He talked about his brother having to join the army because there are no opportunities for young men in the US. I asked him what his own aspirations were, and he said, 'Keep my head down, work the bars, sell a bit of blow on the side and maybe one day I'll have my own bar.'

We walked to get a breakfast burrito and he went back to Oakland on the BART flipping me a departing, 'If you get horny call me.'

Horny? I'd have to be on a self-destruct mission to call him.

147

Saturday 12th March

I had a few clients this morning, some of which are mirroring the same situation I am going through with Jax, and it's often the case that your clients link with you somehow. I have been working with one woman who has been left with some self-esteem issues after her marriage ended. She has this vision of what it is to be a 'good girl,' a blueprint coming from her grandmother that 'good girls' don't like sex. So she had somehow managed to marry a sexless man. They didn't have kids and now in her thirties, her hormones are kicking in and she wants sex all of the time. She was confused as to why from nothing, she is leaning over tables in coffee shops and pushing her vagina into the corner of the table, just to get some kind of relief from the stimulation on her clitoris. She doesn't know if she wants children, but now with this new lover who is ten years younger than her, she is making some dumb sexual health and contraception decisions. She is in a cycle of guilt about wanting sex, guilt that he is so young, guilt about paying for hotels in the town where she lives, guilt about her ex-husband.

We worked back to the first moment she felt this guilt, and it was at her grandmother's house when she lifted up her skirt to show her knickers through the fence to the boy next door. The boy, even though he was older and knew what he was asking her to do, didn't get into trouble, she did. She was told 'good girls don't show their knickers', and felt this horrible guilt that she had corrupted the boy. Then she was sent to a religious school that taught her how bad Eve was for giving Adam the apple. Somehow this story was not the metaphor for her skirt lifting. There is no spiritual voice that comes out of any religion for women; apart from, perhaps, paganism and that is viewed as a sexual religion with horned gods and horny goddesses. If you like it, you're a slut, if you don't like it you're frigid.

I wrote my book for the women of our time, a place where teenage boys grow up watching women in eye-wateringly painful porn films and think that stuff is the norm. Women now need to have self-esteem more than ever to be able to have a sexual voice that is sensual and about pleasure rather than a test of endurance.

I enjoy talking to clients and I like this one very much. Most of the healing comes from the laugh we have together about the whole thing. I'm often so tempted to tell her 'OMG MEEE TOOO' in a session, but the training in coaching has taught me better than to do that.

Carol, my boss at Green Café called me today too. She's very excited because she has been given the contract to green a new café/bakery that's opening. As soon as she told me that it already exists but they are moving premises, I knew it was the one where Jax used to work. She was really happy as the money from this would secure Green Café's future for another six months, and she asked me if I'd consider extending my visa if she wrote a letter to the immigration department. I went along with the idea and said I would look into it. She has a meeting with the owner of the coffee shop in their old place later today before the move and asked me if I would go with her. As I know there is no possible way Jax would be there, I went along.

The place was amazing. There was a whole wall just devoted to cupcakes, beautifully presented like art forms. The whole layout made you become slightly aroused just by the smell of sugar and it was like stepping into *Willy Wonka's Chocolate Factory*. The baristas and waiting staff seemed to glide across the floor. All of them beautiful people, all of them looking identical in the uniforms, trim bodies pushed pertly up against thin cotton. They all looked the same, as if they were guitar players in the iconic 'Addicted to Love' video.

I could see why Jax didn't fit in here. The woman who owns the place told us that she has big dreams for the move. She wants a more profitable demographic, with less coffee shops in that area and a more French line of pastries. 'Cupcakes are yesterday's news,' she said.

I can imagine how she sacked Jax, in one of those sentences where you say nothing but it sounds really pretty. 'It's been so beautiful having you are part of our team but we feel intuitively that your path is in another direction, thank you for playing.' It's the kind of thing you can only get away with in America.

This is a place where everyone is always 'excited'. 'I'm so excited to meet you!' translates to a British person as ecstatic. We would say, 'I'm happy to meet you'. So to be excited to meet me I would have to be Bill Gates about to offer you a million-dollar job. I didn't dislike her for it, but I couldn't leave it without saying something. I had to bring it up.

'I think a guy I know used to work here, do you know Jaxson?' I asked.

'Sure, Jaxson was here up until a few weeks ago, he didn't want to work out his notice,' she said.

'So you didn't want to take him to the new place,' I asked.

'No we needed to make some cuts to make the move and Jaxson was unreliable and didn't fit into the brand.'

Strange, he'd always left my bed on time to get to work, but I guess that he might not have done that every morning. I could see why his big bearded face didn't fit in with the sleekness of this place. I thought it was only models that built advertising brands, but it seems brand is the whole thing. Sex sells and the waiting staff here are worth drooling over, even if the cupcakes are yesterday's news.

Facebook tells me Jax has vanished off to stay with his dad somewhere in California.

I feel connected with him by reading his posts and the songs he puts up on his YouTube homepage.

I am going through such an intense shifting process right now. I feel as if the book has been a magic shifting tool. I expected it to be that for other people, but I don't think I realised the power of writing it for myself. I have been looking for a few answers in the same people who drove me into coming to America. I have found the answers by logging into myself and hearing what I have to say. I know now that I need a stable place where I feel secure and from that place I can travel and do my work all over the world. That place has always felt as if it would have love in it, in terms of a partner. I have always thought that home is a person rather than a place. I expected to come to San Francisco, find my person and see this place as being my home. This hasn't happened. All my life I thought America would end up being my home; it is so confusing to find that I no longer think it is.

No matter how hard you need to try or not try, I am not feeling the flow here. I feel this period of my life in San Francisco is about creating what I need to give birth to, to bring to the world and then the job is over. It feels there is a strong purpose in being here even though I am not completely clear on what that is. I'll know with the 20/20 vision of hindsight. The safety I am looking for now, seems to be for the dog. So she has people who can take care of her when I need to work. That support isn't here.

I confided in Nat and admitted that I am worried that by the end of this year, I still won't know where home is and where I want to be. It's never been London and I have always wanted to live in the States. So I have never considered any place else. Now I am, I have too, I can't think of anywhere else I can be. I am waiting to find the rock I can connect with in the stormy sea.

The greatest question is the one that is still in my future. It's the one where I get to look back on the choices I made, and how that feels in the aftermath of my decision. Without a family, will I ever feel like I have a home? Opposed to if I do have a family will I feel trapped? The answer to both of those questions is yes and no at the same time. It is a long life ahead and terribly short. It's long to live in regret and short when you run out of options. I need love to help make up my mind for me.

Monday 14th March

I had another dream about my schoolgirl crush, Mark. This time it was a situation that happened in real life. At school I always knew where he was. Our school was split into blocks, each distinguished by a letter. If I were in C block I would know he was in A block. My friend Katie and I would always walk from block to block looking for the boys we fancied. She was always amazed that I knew where he was.

When I was sixteen and still living at home, I used to ride a motorbike to get around and had a job as a washer-up in a restaurant. This particular night, work had been horrible because I'd had to gut fifty fish. So I thought about Mark to keep my mind off what I was doing. After the shift I felt a pull to ride my bike past the top of his road. It was about 1 a.m. in the morning. As I turned the corner, he was crossing the road with his dog heading for the beach. I pulled over and asked if he wanted some company. This is where the dream started. He told me he couldn't sleep as he was thinking about me. We walked across a golf course and onto the beach where we found a bench to sit on. It was pitch black, but he knew where he was going.

Now in reality, nothing happened because I was freezing cold and was convinced I smelt of the corpses of fifty fish. But in dreamland the outcome was different and we started kissing. It was so clear in the dream I could even remember his smell. He pushed me back gently until I was lying down on the bench. I am wearing my school uniform (in reality, you can't wear a skirt and tights on a motorbike). He lifted my skirt and started to roll his fingers over my clit through my tights. He started to pull them down, and took them just far enough down so that he could slip his tongue through the gap – but before he'd even pulled my tights and pants down over my butt cheeks I woke up.

Frustrated I slipped my fingers between my legs, the dream had made me so wet I was pushing my hips into the mattress. I finished myself off and rolled over and went back to sleep.

In the morning the dream was still in my head, so I checked Facebook and read Jax's page, which is turning into the morning papers! I read that he is planning to move back to Seattle to stay with his family for a while. I thought it would be me who would leave to go back to the UK. I am annoyed with him for giving up so easily. His update read:

> I went to school in Idaho for a year and got punched in the face by life then I moved back to Seattle and got punched in the face by life and then I moved to San Francisco and got punched in the face by life and now that my face is numb to the pain and I'm not afraid any more, I'm slowly making my way back to Seattle where the weed is greener.

Weed is greener? Well that might explain his lateness and the fact he seemed to be ill all the time. Maybe he didn't want to see me when he was stoned! He can't even see that he is the one creating his life. It makes me feel so sad that someone with such potential is willing to let himself go. I have seen it before. I guess many times through my life, I've seen that it's easier to blame something or someone else rather than yourself. For some people that never stops. Even if I called him and tried to wake him up, it would look like I had an invested interest. I know I need to let him to contact me – if he ever will. However, with my upcoming trip to Seattle, I'll have to tell him I'll be in town.

It would be great to spend time with him in another city, and might even be worth booking into a really nice hotel. I love hotels; I find them a really creative place to work, as well as being really sexy. Something about crisp white linen, Egyptian cotton sheets makes them feel cool on naked skin. I think about making love with Jax in one of those oversized hotel showers, where I can use the handrail to support my body while my legs are wrapped around his waist. The water cascading down over us, getting in my mouth, rushing down between my breasts and over his cock as it pulls out only to push back in…Don't get me started on hotels with a steam room. Hotels are places of fantasy were you don't have to be who you are and no one knows. I think got this hotel fantasy thing from talking to one of my clients.

I know Jax and I are over, but maybe for just one last night! I really hope Jax will be in Seattle at the same time as me.

Nat is now fully into the guy who lives in the Tenderloin. Turns out he's loaded but really tight with money. They go to all the best places, but then split the bill. It's easy for him to pay for fish and chips in a top restaurant, but Nat can really only stretch to eating it out of the bag. She has suggested that they take it in turns to arrange where to go. So she took him to a really nice place called Delancey Street Restaurant on the Embarcadero where the food and service is amazing, and it's really cheap. Former substance abusers, ex-convicts and homeless people staff the whole place. He thought she was being really socially conscious and loved it.

However, her big plan about making it clear that she doesn't have the income for a $30 fillet of plaice didn't go down so well. She asked me what could she do to tell him that she isn't on the same pay scale as him. Of course there is only one answer, which is to tell him, as he'll find out eventually – or get more clients. She's decided to try and get more clients!

Friday 18th March

Jax seems to have fallen off the Facebook planet. There hasn't been an update from him for a while. I know he was living with his dad and he might have moved back to Seattle. So I popped him an email to tell him I was coming into town to do the radio interview and spend a few days. No reply yet.

I have treated myself and booked a nice hotel room. Whether he's in it or not, I think a few days holiday are just what I need right now. I've been working really hard promoting the book. Not once in any of the interviews has anyone asked me about my love life. I haven't felt like a self-help fraud in any of them. I have also been writing articles and, as it turns out, the relationship with Jax has been a very good muse for my writing. I wrote an article about how to control anxiety when he doesn't get back to you. It was a really powerful piece and was published by a popular online newspaper.

I have been controlling my anxiety too. I know it's over but would just like to see him one last time. I think if I'm honest it's sexually motivated. I find it really hard to go from an active sex life to just being cold turkey giblets. It's not even about the sex itself, it's about the connection I feel when I am with him. I learnt from being with Dean that night that it's not about the sex. Dean was exciting technically accurate sex, but I felt nothing – well nothing really good anyway. There is something I am looking for in these sexual connections. I'm definitely in search of something otherwise I wouldn't have written a book about it. I've decided it's all Facebook's fault and being part of the crossover generation.

When I was at school we had a computer room with about five computers. They tried to give us all typing lessons, which I thought was pointless unless you wanted to be a secretary and I didn't because I couldn't spell. There were no mobile phones. In my lifetime, the way we communicate has totally changed.

I still carry a paper diary when I have all of that available on my smart phone. You never have to say anything difficult face to face anymore because texting keeps you at a safe distance. The only total sod happens when the other person doesn't reply to a text or an email or return your call immediately. Then there is 'radio silence' and we worry that radio silence will go on and on and on. Just like having a radio station on in the background whilst you're cleaning the house or doing other stuff, you don't really hear it until it goes off. The radio presenter doesn't get back from the bathroom in time for the end of the song, or you lose transmission in the middle of a news report. You weren't really listening but now the radio silence is deafening. It's the same as when you're waiting for a call or a message. You don't know how long you'll have to wait and all the paranoid reasons why they might not be getting back to you start to crowd into your mind.

There is a fabulous story by Dorothy Parker called *A Telephone Call* and there's a part when she thinks that him being dead is a better solution for her than him not calling. I smile every time I read it and I read it to remember what a crock of ridiculousness us women create for the fear of feeling empty. Men focus on one thing at a time and if we are not the centre of their thoughts, we think there is something wrong with us. If Dorothy Parker was writing in the age of mobile phones, I think she would have found one of her options in her poem *Resumé* a little more interesting! That fact that not everything is automatic, you are automatically disappointed, when for all you know he just sat on the loo!

Friday 25th March

If sourdough bread is the heart of San Francisco then coffee runs through the veins of Seattle. From the ninth floor of the Mayflower Park Hotel, I swear I can still smell the coffee in the streets below. My nostrils, and the tiny hairs inside of them, seem to be caked in the brown liquid, in the same way that carbon from the cars creates black bogeys in London. Starbucks outgrew its mother and took over not only Seattle's finest coffee shops, but also the world.

I would like to say that I see Jax's face here in all of the young men that pass me on the street. However, I can no longer recall his face, just his energetic presence when it was upbeat happy and connected to me. The Jax that Seattle knows, the one that grew up here, I'm not sure exists any more. I think he will come back a changed man, when he does come back. That's if, he's not here now because he never emailed me back. I seem to understand both Jax and Kurt Cobain so much better just walking around their hometown.

Each city has its story and every person is touched by the history of the place. In the same way that we inherit our family's belief system, which is based on our ancestors that have gone before, a city has the same capacity. In order to fit in, you have to become like the other people who live there. It's like stepping in with a certain vibe. If you can't step in you don't fit in and it only leads to loneliness. Of course, this is true of entire countries and cultures too, but in cities you don't expect it. You think you can be who you are and the city will change into being what it is. A large corporation like Starbucks moulds the city. We become what are sold.

The people I have met so far here don't seem to be as nice as in California. Maybe they are not as fake, but there is definitely no hiding that they can't stand tourists. I remember feeling like that when I was growing up living by the sea in Ireland and, then again as a teenager, in Somerset. However, I imagine living somewhere like Seattle it must be worse. In fact, I noticed it in London too. The slowness of the tourists, as they walk through the ticket barriers and stop like bovine cattle walking into a slaughterhouse. It was one of the things about living there that started to make me hate myself, as the place seemed to inspire my impatience and intolerance.

Understanding what home means is terribly complex. Home can only really be the people you resonate with. And I guess for some that is only going to be the place that they grew up in. But for people like me, who moved around a lot as a child, it is easy to feel a sense of disconnect. What's interesting is I believe that I am a jigsaw piece that connects with more places and more people *because* of my diverse life. But it means that fewer people connect with me.

I have decided that sleeping in a posh hotel with soft cotton sheets and pillows, which melt from the weight of your cheeks, is a sad luxury when you're single. There is something that is such a turn on about crushing crisp white sheets. Like taking somebody's virginity, the newness is never the same again once slept on. It's a beautiful moment, when you pull back the sheets for the first time and see the clean white untouched softness. It's for that reason alone that posh hotel rooms are so seductive, coupled with the fact that it's not you that has to return the sheets back to what they were. This is the life that I wanted to live; this is the life that I'm living. I don't have to live it all the time because if I did it wouldn't feel special. Just those one-off moments when you find that deal on the Internet and it allows you to play out a role of financial success.

Saturday 26th March

The radio interview went really well. I spent some time looking round the city and took a coffee in the first ever Starbucks, which looks more like a museum that serves coffee.

I booked a table for one at the restaurant at the top of the Space Needle and now, sitting with my face almost pressed up against the moving glass, I don't feel sad. In fact, I am overwhelmed with pride at how far I have come. From London – sitting with my neighbour drinking wine watching *Grey's Anatomy* – to now, drinking wine in the same place that is the focal point of the beginning of each episode. It is a romantic place. The drama queen in me would love to have a melancholic turnaround and feel sad to be a single woman having dinner alone. In the distance, the mountains are clear and I know I have climbed so far in my lifetime. I am so grateful to have been born into a culture and a body that has made it possible for me to fuck up and find joy all at the same time.

I don't think I expected the move to San Francisco to stay being such a trip. I think I thought it would stop at some point. The biggest journey is the one I have taken with my past and myself. I see the future so much more clearly now. It feels calmer and do-able. It feels like a very beautiful place to be. Not so different from the place I am now. I see it with a sustainable home. I know I am about two years from this. I also know that the next two years will be some work. They feel successful; they feel like I will have the space for love – which I haven't had thus far.

When I was in a long-term relationship with Simon, I found the idea of Internet dating exciting. When you're in a relationship, there isn't the same risk. The prospect of getting to know someone you have never met and the feeling of hopeful expectation. The very first Internet date I had in San Francisco, only happened after I spent ages sending emails back and forth with the same guy. In fact, it was such a protracted process that I started to wonder whether he would ever ask me out on a date. Eventually he did in a roundabout way. He said that he wished that we could meet in a more spontaneous way, like bumping into each other on the street or in some kind of James Bond scene.

I took the bait and sent him an email:

Your mission, if you choose to accept it (OK, wrong film, but same idea – fast-paced action heroes!) is to go to the Ferry Building, to The Slanted Door bar at 7 p.m. and pick up your instructions from the bartender.

M.

He simply wrote back:

OK, M. Will do.

I got myself to the bar at 6.30 p.m. I asked the barman if I could leave a box with him to be collected. In the box was a note that read:

Go to the end of Pier 1 and bring ice.

M.

I had packed a flask of vodka martini with olives and two plastic martini glasses. By 7.30 p.m. he still hadn't arrived and I was getting cold. At 7.45 p.m. he sent a text saying that he couldn't find Pier 1.

Common sense would tell you, even if you didn't see the large writing that said 'Pier 1', that it might be the first pier and, indeed, the one closest to the bar, so the ice wouldn't melt. I put the note in a box so he could use the box to bring the ice. In fact, I had done all the thinking for him, he really only needed to put a few clues together.

He turned up all flustered, saying how wonderful this was and how no one had ever been that inventive or sweet to him before. He had ice, but not in the box that I had left with the barman for it. But in a Starbucks cup. He had gone all the way to Starbucks because the barman wouldn't give him a glass and he didn't think to put it into the box.

When I put the ice in the glasses and began to pour the vodka martinis he had a bit of a panic, and said, 'You do know it's illegal to drink outside in San Francisco, right?'

So I had to come up with a contingency plan to make him feel safe, which was that if the police came all the way down to the end of the pier, then we could pour the drinks into the bay. We stood by the rail, just in case, to ease his troubled mind. At this point, perhaps, I should have made the connection that San Francisco might not be the romantic place I had envisioned.

Sunday 27th March

When I arrived back in San Francisco a distraught Nat met me at the airport. Her Tender Knob fella had ended it because he'd decided she was out for his money. We headed to the Batman Bar at the top of the Marriott and downed some martinis, which gave me a hankering memory of my date with Jax. I paid, as Nat was now really skint from trying to keep up with Mr Knob Head.

Luckily it was table service, so I didn't have to confront the bartender who had seen me with my knickers stuffed in my hand trying to find change. I told Nat what had happened and she couldn't believe I was so brazen in such a posh bar. You can only be brazen in a posh bar, if you're brazen in a cheap bar you'd be classed as a slut. Whore in a cheap hotel room, prostitute or hooker in a posh one, no matter what the client is paying.

A little worst for wear, I stumbled into the flat later. I'd been so good and not checked Jax's Facebook page the whole time I'd been in Seattle. I had checked email, of course, just in case.

The headline sobered me up quickly:

Been to the doctor and its bipolar 1 disorder. Prescribed to start with 200mg of LAMICTAL every night before I go to bed. Staying strong. I'm smart, resilient, bipolar, worst motherfucking nightmare.

I looked up bipolar 1 disorder online on Wikipedia and started reading:

> One of the most severe forms of mental illness, bipolar 1 disorder is characterised by recurrent episodes of mania and (more often) depression. The condition has a high rate of recurrence and, untreated, has an approximately 15 per cent risk of death by suicide.

I don't get it? Would I have not known?

My cheeks start to flush red. I don't know if I am angry, embarrassed or guilty. I can't believe it. Then my head starts justifying and rushing through every conversation we ever had, as everything I know about him suddenly becomes repositioned and redefined. I'm looking for clues, I don't know if I am looking for clues that it isn't true, or for clues that it is. It boils down to this: pot smoking, twenty-one-year-old trying to make it in life. Not getting enough sleep due to his silly working hours then loses his job and gets depressed.

Let's face it US doctors are known to medicate any problem – even those that are a normal part of being a person. Highs and lows, we all get them. How can this be true? Why did I not see this coming? How could I have missed it? Could I be the cause? Then I swing back to thinking it's not true again. It's just another way that Jax has found to self-sabotage his life's purpose because the enormity of his talents feels too much. I am a rescuer. I save people as relationship insurance. I wouldn't have missed this.

I feel like Jax is a bird falling from the sky and I am swooping down to save him, but not so fast that I'll hit the ground myself. He is a twenty-one-year-old guy pissed off at life. Lost his job, he has a hard time because he is a creative genius with no direction for it. He isn't mentally ill he's just lost. Then what do I know? I have hardly had any time with him and, the truth is, he has acted a little different each time, but then he is an American! I can feel myself wanting to take it all on, so he doesn't have too. The pain of missing him now is extreme and I don't have time to focus on it.

Tuesday 29th March

It's pretty late but Jax has posted the saddest doctored photo of himself holding his meds on his Facebook page this evening. It seems to be a really private thing to announce over a social network. It's almost as if he thinks he is a rock star documenting his own demise.

I send him an email and try really hard not to mess with his head.

> Sorry to hear about how you're feeling. I've never been a fan of medication, but I know you will do what you feel is best. I hope you were really open with the doctor so his observations are really correct.
>
> Thinking of you.
>
> Sam

Then I go to bed. Somehow I am asleep before my head hits the pillow. Deep dreams again, this time Mark is holding out a hand and saying to me, 'It's time to come home.' But I can't reach his hand, as my legs won't move properly. There is no power in them and it feels like I am trying to wade through treacle.

In the dream, he is beautiful like a blue-eyed angel in

white. I hope this isn't a prediction of my own death? Or I'm about to find out that Mark is dead? I'm reading way too much into this dream! I don't think the Mark in my dreams has anything to do with him as a person.

Wednesday 30th March

This morning I told Anna about Jax. She said that stuff is easy for people to hide, and they often do. It seems in America, if you don't have some kind of mental health disorder or aren't taking meds for something, then you're not fully living!

She was far more interested in my latest dream. She thinks Mark is an archetypal messenger from my subconscious. She wanted to know if there were patterns in my waking life that he could be representing. In my dreams, we are always going to have sex, but then we never do. She asked me how I feel about not having sex with him. I told her, I felt heartbroken – like it was an emotional loss.

Often these dreams happen in my waking life too, when I need to be really strong. Which might be why I am having more of them now I am living in the States, I'm on my own here.

Anna thinks the dreams might be about self-love. I thought I had done a lot of work on self-love and personal values. After all, I am an expert in that, and got a little defensive with her. But maybe there is more to go. Anna described it being like layers, often when you heal one thing then the next thing underneath shows up. She might be right.

I didn't expect it, but when I turned on Facebook there was a message from Jax:

> Thanks buddy, I think I'll be good as long as this medicine doesn't cause a full body rash. I've got some work and family around to occupy a lot of my time, and the baseball season is coming up =) but it gets pretty bad sometimes. My left frontal cortex is all out of whack and I am having a hard time managing my emotions, but I know I'm not alone thanks to da supafriendz like you!

I don't know what's worse, him having a mental illness or calling me 'buddy' and 'supafriendz'. The good news is that I can put that down to his mental illness! The bad news is, we are just friends. It's a clear 'back off I don't need you'. If I can't be part of the solution, I will become part of the problem. So backing off is a very good idea!

Thursday 31st March

I think might be addicted to hurting myself and am suffering pain by Facebook. Jax is having a very public breakdown, or cry for attention, and is splatting it all over the Internet. It's an angry 'fuck you this is who I am rant', but proclaiming himself as 'This is the moron I am, fuck you if you think I'm a loser' is really not really him, because he's not a moron!

He told me a lot of his posts on Facebook are propaganda (although he didn't use those terms). I wonder if my own mental health would be better if I stopped checking his page. I get a pain behind my ribs when I read the things he is saying.

He has started filming himself too. Sometimes he doesn't say anything; he just looks at the camera like he is staring down at the world. I don't see him behind his eyes. You know you love the person, but the person looking back at you isn't the person you love.

Facebook gives me the time he posted his 'pain' and it makes me feel connected to the very second he is falling – yet there is nothing I can do to catch him. If someone falls under a bus in front of you, you see it and can react. This is happening in the same moment, I can see it and there is nothing I can do. Honestly I love myself for feeling this way; I find it funny, endearing and pathetic all at the same time.

I have three clients today and am giving a workshop on 'Finding Your Next Love'. My life is a good metaphor for people who are scared to fly; I am scared to land. I feel as though being in States has given me the chance to be in other people's spaces and use their lives to reflect upon my own. I didn't expect to be so close to forty and living like this.

Although I have released myself from contemplating that this is my last chance to have a child. I have reached a final conclusion for the time being on that subject. I had thought that I had some deep psychological reason for not wanting a child. I realise, however, that I've been thinking about it without having all the information. The biggest part that's missing, of course, is a partner. For me, it's pointless to think about even entering into motherhood without one. So if I decide I want a child then I'd get the right father without any problem, which would imply some kind of control over love. It isn't me who will decide if I want a child. It is will be us deciding to build a family.

This isn't a part of this life; this would be a new life. I am not in that new life; I may not find the new life. I guess I knew this but thought if I came to America then a new life would start in this new place and a man would be part of the package. No wonder I was surprised when it didn't work out the way I had it in my mind.

Friday 1st April

Today was one of Jax's worst Facebook films. He hasn't posted any for a while. I thought that might be because he's moved out of his dad's place and didn't have a webcam. Even better, I'd hoped it was because he didn't feel that he needed to make them. In this last three-minute film you rarely see the top of his head (it's covered by his hands with the base of his palms in his eye sockets) as he rocks backwards and forwards. Talking sometimes in rhyme, sometimes quite funny, but mostly in desperate pain about his loneliness and his inability to climb out of the rabbit hole that he feels he's in. If the medication isn't working, it's probably because it's medicating the wrong thing and he isn't bipolar. Although I don't really feel this is important any more. All I can see is the man reaching out.

I showed Nat his Facebook page and the films. She thinks he's acting and just crying out for attention. But who does that? I have no idea if any of his friends on Facebook are reaching back or watching his public display of a man breaking down, as though it is some episode of *Big Brother*. I miss him and can see that the person on the screen bears no resemblance to the man I had in my bed. I don't know what my responsibility is in this. My whole body just wants to help, just wants to make him better.

It's not within my power and he probably wouldn't let me anyway.

After watching the film, I cracked and sent him a text message, just telling him that my friendship is there for him. All he has to do is reach me and I'll be there. With my whole heart I believe that I can actually fix him, but I have to admit that this last film has scared me. He looks completely mentally ill. Still, somehow, I think I have some kind of magic wand that will be able to fix him. In truth, he is paying me the greatest kindness by not letting me try and help him. I think somehow connections go much deeper than one lifetime. You can't explain how you know, you just know.

In the film, some of things Jax said seem to echo my own experience. He talks about wanting to make a new start, find a home, and that's exactly what I thought he was doing in San Francisco. But, perhaps, living in the big city – although only forty-eight miles away – was too much for him.

I was also the person expecting to find a sense of home in San Francisco and often find it too much. And when he said, 'I just want to reach out to you to let you know that you're not the only person suffering with loneliness,' I felt as if he were speaking to me personally.

Jax seems to be facing the human condition with more authenticity than most people ever dare. But I'm still not sure whether he was brave or stupid to put it all on Facebook. It must really be hurting his family and I can't believe that they are not checking the wall as often, if not more, than I am.

Tuesday 5th April

Within one dog walk, I have decided to leave San Francisco. As I was crossing the road from Guerrero to turn down 18th, there was a man wearing a Greenpeace T-shirt and holding a clipboard jumping up and down. In front of him, in the gutter, was an old Chinese man collecting flyers that he had dropped. His body movements showed that these actions were causing him pain. People walked past him on the crossing. I checked the seconds of time available before the lights changed and collected the flyers that had flown onto the crossing. As I was still picking them up, the man with a Greenpeace T-shirt asked me if I care about the environment.

I took a moment.

I wanted to say to him that he is oblivious to the environment he is in. A young man with enough energy to jump around with a clipboard doesn't have enough energy or time to help an old man clean up the very environment right in front of him. But I just said, 'I care about this man right now.'

He ignored my comment and continued looking for more passers by.

As I walked, I was struck not for the first time how beautiful this part of San Francisco is, the buildings are gorgeous backed by a blue sky, offered in various colours of paint. At pavement cafés there were people drinking glasses of wine in the sunshine. Long lines of people were waiting to devour organic ice cream at the Bi-Rite. Everyone seemed to be smiling. I stopped to look at some clothes at a garage sale on the street. There were five well-dressed girls-about-town types with perfect hair and Audrey Hepburn sunglasses. I went to look at a dress and, somehow, while moving the dress along, the rail collapsed in my hand. I turned to my audience of beautiful people, laughed in slight embarrassment and said, 'It wasn't me, I didn't touch it, I wasn't even anywhere near it,' in almost a *Little Britain* style of comedy.

They didn't laugh; they just looked at me like I had dropped out of another planet to piss all over their party. I offered to help the girl put the rail back together while the other girls stood and watched. The woman didn't even talk to me or interact with me while I held one end of the rail to stop the clothes falling off. It was as if I were a nuisance. So I felt I had to justify the fact that the rail broke, that it wasn't my fault and anyone who had moved an item of clothing at that point would have had the rail collapse. She didn't acknowledge that I was even speaking.

Since first arriving in San Francisco Dolores Park has held a fascination for me. It's like being in one of the art spaces at Glastonbury Festival. I always believed that if I ever felt like I belonged in Dolores Park in the summer, then I would feel like I belonged in San Francisco. It's a beautiful park with a lovely view of the city. And so much goes on in this space, people doing yoga, people naked sunbathing, drug addicts foaming at the mouth, the hash truffle man balancing his brass pots of truffles over both shoulders, the Mexican man pushing his ice-cream cart, a strange girl who takes her own chair and sits in it rocking backwards and forwards, and the young hipsters getting drunk from brown-paper-wrapped bottles of alcohol. This is not the park life that Blur wrote about.

I discovered Dolores Park by accident, within the first few weeks of exploring my new neighbourhood, and decided in that moment that this would be where I would have my birthday party.

I wanted to have a picnic for my birthday because my birthday falls in May, which is often too cold in the UK for an outside event. So last May I had a picnic in the park. It started at 2 p.m. but the first guest didn't arrived until an hour later. This is very Californian, although I didn't know that at the time. It is very normal for people to turn up two hours late and think nothing of it.

Looking at the park, I feel ready to leave. I think it would be wrong to be with this opportunity to make something of myself in America and only stay in one place. The Americans change from area to area, so who knows whether I would fit in a little better somewhere else.

Wednesday 6th April

Dean sent me an email out of the blue today asking if I wanted to meet up and whether I still had his number. I let him know he wasn't deleted and I was in San Francisco. In reply, he asked if I could meet him after 11 p.m. I was already meeting some friends that night in the 500 Club, so I asked him to meet with me there. It felt strange meeting him in the place that I'd waited for Jax. Dean saw me before I saw him. He came up behind me, wrapped his arms around my waist and kissed the nape of my neck. It felt comforting. Being a bartender, he ordered some crazy concoction that we were going to drink as a shot. That drink on top of the three vodka tonics I now was drunk.

Dean was very friendly, like he was pleased to see me and seemed more connected to me than he had been before. He told me a little bit more about his confusion about being mixed race. He doesn't like the fact that people don't see him as being black and that he could have come from anywhere. He also confessed that he sells pot. It's interesting to me that even though he doesn't look black he is trying very hard to fit into a negative black stereotype. Which included this pick-you-up and drop-it-down attitude he has to our sexual connection.

This time in the bedroom he just seemed to be so focused on himself. I got really bored with giving him head and was reaching a point where I just wanted the whole thing to be over. I couldn't understand why I was here again!

It really sucks when you hit that point when you fake an orgasm. But I wasn't getting anywhere close to even being able to pretend that I was going to have an orgasm, it was all about him. We're about to have penetrative sex for the third time, and I thought that this would be a good point to end it if he hadn't cum after that. His total determination to cum seemed kind of weird and he was clearly frustrated when he couldn't climax. Some of that frustration was being vented on my body. In the way he gripped my arms, back of my head or held my hips. I almost didn't dare move.

I unwrapped and handed him the condom took a swig of water and assumed the brace position. I was thinking to myself that I just want to be in a relationship where I can be honest and just say, 'Hey I'm done can we resume in the morning?'

When two people are mutually using each other then you really take care of your own needs during sex. As he pushed into me, nothing felt different, but something had changed in him. I couldn't figure out what it was. I found myself just reacting to his cock, I pulled away, turned round to face him and immediately saw he wasn't wearing the condom. He only got a thrust or two in, but a wave of panic hit me. I held myself and trying not to sound too shaky asked him, 'Where's the condom?'

'I don't know,' he said.

I checked the bed then myself but I couldn't find it. He tried to move me into the second sexual position very subtly.

'You didn't put it on did you?'

'No I didn't.'

The blood rushed to my face, the shaking came from shoulders and reverberated around my hands. My stomach turned over tied itself into a knot and the reflux of acid from the alcohol burned my tonsils.

'It's OK,' he said. 'Look, I've been to the doctor and I'm firing blanks.'

'It's not fucking OK with me! It's not about getting pregnant, it's nothing to do with getting pregnant and everything to do with safe sex, what the fuck were you thinking.'

'You're not likely to get HIV this way,' he said dismissively.

'It's not your choice to make. You don't get to choose how I look after my sexual health. You don't get to decide if I want to use a condom. Just who do you think you are?'

He then said if I carried on this conversation, he would leave. It's an emotional blackmail technique, they assume that you don't want them to leave and it's nice to sleep next to them. I informed him that I would love him to leave but it was a stupid threat to make. He'd never get back to Oakland at 2.30 a.m. in the morning without a car. He then pretended to be asleep. I lay there in bed wondering how I got here with my anger building up. Then when I realised he actually was going to sleep as his breathing changed I truly understood he didn't give a fuck about me and if I lay here with him in my bed then I didn't give a fuck about me ether. With my whole body shaking I got out of bed, pulled back the covers and said, 'OUT!'

'What? Seriously, you're kicking me out for that?'

'Out! Get out of my room, I want you out!'

'No.'

'Get out!'

'No.'

There is something that comes over a woman when a man invades her space, it's a kind of energy rape, and a women will freeze or fight and I have only ever gone into fight mode.

'You get out of my bed and out of my room or I am going to disintegrate you.'

'Disintegrate me, who says that! You're not on *Dr Who*.'

Then Dean looked me in the eyes for the first time and sat up fully in the bed. 'OK I'm sorry, I'm sorry I didn't put a condom on, but seriously don't you think you're being a bit hysterical?'

Why is it that when a woman states what she wants she is being hysterical? I used my very best quiet psycho voice, which comes with its own built-in Cockney accent. This is the voice that comes out when I feel threatened or in a situation where I am about to be attacked. It's slow, calm and very intimidating.

'You are leaving now, I'm not 'aving any more fuckin' conversation with you, do you understand me? Get your shit out of my room.'

In a childish strop he moved around the room collecting his stuff. I had stopped shaking now and watched him like a predator looking at its kill. He avoided my eyes, but I could see the goose bumps on his skin as my energy melted his entire smartarse attitude right out of him.

'How am I supposed to get home,' he said like a sulky child talking to his mother.

'You're not my problem.'

Throwing me a hard stare, Dean walked out of the door. I waited to hear the front door close and then the metal gate at the bottom of the steps, before I flopped onto the bed and began to feel the first stage of my hangover head start to kick in.

You're not my problem.

I started to realise that one of my big problems in life is not being able to tell the difference between what's my problem and some else's. What made me so angry about Dean's not using a condom wasn't just a safe sex issue. It's that my rule of myself had been broken.

When I closed my eyes, I could see Dean's torso overprinted with the face of every man who has ever used sex as a form of power and disrespect, and which I didn't have enough respect for myself to stop. He had broken the floodgates of my un-dealt-with grief and sadness, and it was manifesting as anger and rage in my heart. I wasn't angry with those men, I was angry with me.

The next day, I sent him an email telling him that he owed himself and, certainly me, more respect and that I didn't want his name to flash up on my phone again. Of course he did what any psycho would, he called me that night at 1.15 a.m. I didn't pick up and he left a message trying to sound ambiguous about our situation, as though it were just a hitch, a misunderstanding and that I would come round.

Thursday 28th April

Dean sent another text today saying he would be in San Francisco at 11 p.m. I know he got the email that I sent a couple or so weeks ago, and this is just bullshit to get the upper hand. So, I called him on it and sent him a text:

> I know you got the email, if you have something to say I'll hear it, but I have nothing to say to you. Sam

His reply:

> ?

So I called him on it again.

> You can't play me, I know what I know, and you got the email, now we are done.

Of course he sent a reply acting like this is all news to him – again. My heart right now feels shut; I don't feel anything about his email.

I took a trip to the doctor a couple of weeks ago, not about a shut heart but to see about getting a STD check-up after the stupid condom episode. She told me that faking putting a condom on is common in San Francisco, and many people become HIV positive that way.

'The thing you need to know about San Francisco,' she said, 'is that even the straight boys sleep with gay guys, so you need to be on the lookout for yourself here.'

It all underlined my decision to leave San Francisco. And, as it turns out, it didn't take much to undo.

After giving notice on the flat, I booked a flight for the dog and me, and then gave away all the stuff I'd acquired. In a few days' from now I'll be gone too – all done in a matter of weeks. The hardest part will be saying goodbye to Nat and Anna. They have both been such an integral part of my life for the past two years.

I know I will have to start again in the UK. I'm not quite sure where I'll settle, but I can stay at my parents' place until I work out what to do next. I'm sure people will think that I've failed. There is always an expectation that you will stay in the country you move to. But unless you have lived there, how would you know if it was for you. The amount of hassle to stay in America would only be worth it for an amazing man or a marvellous job. It's time to go home, it feels right.

Sunday 1st May

The fog was too dense to see catch a last glimpse of San Francisco from the window of the airplane. I was glad. I didn't want to shed any more tears. One thing I really like about Americans is that they are not afraid to express how they feel. I have found myself being able to do this more. Sometimes the words stick in my throat, and there is something very British about not being able to tell someone how valuable they are to you.

We don't know how we touch people's lives perhaps until we leave. I was waiting for someone to touch me enough for me to want to stay. Of course, it would have to be a love interest over a friend. Even though the friends I've made have touched me.

Nat came with me to the airport. She was in bits. I have never seen her cry like that. In fact, I have never seen her cry.

LONDON

Tuesday 3rd May

First, I went to meet my friend Kate in London and somehow walking along High Street Kensington, where we were meeting, everything felt different. I was already really enjoying being here again. It surprised me, as I'd never felt it was my place before. There was something reassuring about walking into Boots the Chemist and knowing what all the products were without having to think. It could have been jet lag but it gave me a giddy sense that made me want to laugh while walking down the street.

I noticed that some of the things that I loved about San Francisco had arrived here too – like a wholefoods market and signs about banning of plastic bags in the shops. Listening to the local news in the hotel room, people are talking about rising up and making the government responsible. It feels different here.

London for me is full of ghosts. I remember standing with a boyfriend on Waterloo Bridge looking down on at the National Film Theatre. His name was Peter and he was trying to make a point about how similar we were. He pointed down at the Thames and the riverside, then said, 'What do you see?'

I listed what he expected to hear, I listed what he could see.

He said, 'Exactly.'

But that isn't what I could see. The objects I could see were the backdrop to the ghosts of the people I had lost. I could see a café where I drank coffee with my friend Sarah. I could see the place I stepped out from after seeing the film *Truly Madly Deeply* and couldn't stop crying. I saw my memories, as if they were all taking place at the same time. The more I stay in a place, the more the visions of the past accumulate. London has fifteen years of ghosts for me. San Francisco only has one ghost, Jax. But I feel him here in London too, in the cracks of the pavements and I wish I were walking here with him.

Soon in the chatter of catch-ups with clients and friends, who are likely to ask if I have met Mr Right in San Francisco, I will describe myself as an empowered woman who enjoyed having a toy boy and some fun. I won't talk of the disappointment of my expectation of love, who would want to hear it? I know because in my job, people find me to be an inspiration. It used to make me think that I couldn't mess up because it would let other people down.

I think now being a 'human' I might make an even better coach. I know I have reinvented myself. Reinvention is only possible with an obvious change other people can see. For Madonna, it was a costume or the sound of her music. For me I had to leave and I just wasn't clear what I wanted to say, but I knew that the conversation for me was over. It was time for a new conversation to begin and it started with Kate.

I told her about Jax over coffee and, even as I talked about him, I could feel his presence in my life was no longer there. Not so much geographically, but emotionally, the whole situation felt smaller. I think this must be what getting some perspective on a situation means. When you can see without the drama you have created, that was never really there. I talked about my plan to move to Bristol. Kate was surprised that I didn't want to move back to London. But it's the ghosts I wanted to leave behind and I felt a new start in a new place would serve me much better. If I went back to my old life, it would be as if nothing had happened and it had happened. I had changed and I was a little scared to go back to who I used to be.

Dean showed me how vulnerable I was in America, and even more so without a true support network of family and friends who really have my back or, failing that, the National Health Service. I am a strong independent woman but the game I was playing with Dean was emotionless. It's not that I needed to have emotions for him, but when I put myself in a position where someone's regard or disregard for me counts then I better have balls of steel. I thought those balls were created by being in a place of self-defence but they're not, they are created by being in a place of personal security created of self-belief, self-respect and even self-love. If I really cared for myself would I have put myself in positions where I could have been harmed? It's good to believe the wall I have built around myself will keep me protected. I've come to believe it only really keeps me closed to love. I thought I had a sense of adventure of being able to be brave in the world with the resilience to match. I get it now; my resilience to anything is built not only in personal strength, but also in the support network of friends, family and self-care.

With Dean I thought I was playing one game – 'the sexually empowered independent girl, can play it like the boys', and expecting the prize to be love and appreciation. Advertising being an American footballer without all the padding and then screaming in pain and crying about how unfair it all is when they thump me in the breasts to get the ball. I was playing a game I'm not suited for. Get off the pitch! If the situation with Dean has taught me one thing it's that I need to take care of myself better. It's not even him I am angry with now; it's me for being such a dumb arse for being there in the first place.

There was one thing that I've just remembered, which happened the morning after the first night Dean and I had sex. The dog was on the bed and he was rubbing her belly, I went out to the bathroom and when I came back the dog was in her safe space under the bed. I asked him what was wrong with her. He said she'd been lying on the edge of the bed and when he'd stopped rubbing her belly, she'd just rolled off the edge of the bed as she tried to get up. He went on to say how funny it was.

I asked him, 'Why didn't you stop her falling?'

'I wondered if she would work it out for herself,' was his reply.

I thought at the time this was a total knob head thing to do. The dog could have got hurt and it was just plain nasty. But I did that excessive thinking thing and told myself that maybe he thought she would save herself and didn't mean for her to fall. But the truth is, how you do one thing is how you do everything. At that moment I should have known that he wasn't the kind of person I wanted in my life or my bed.

From this moment forth I've decided will no longer make excuses for what is blatantly obviously shit!

I have always prided myself on being a person that does everything for everyone else. I didn't even really know how to ask for help. My mum made this observation to me once, and says even as a child I never went to anyone for comfort. If I fell over, I just picked myself up and carried on. She said she didn't really know how to mother me, as I wouldn't allow it. I don't know if it's possible to be born into the world not knowing how to be loved.

I have a kind of arrogance and secretly believe that no one will be able to take care of me to my standards. Yet underneath that arrogance there is a softness that really says, 'I don't trust anyone to take care of me.'

Like any belief, you set out in life with, there will be people who will prove you right.

I'm not ignorant of the fact that in Jax I chose to fall in love with a young man with issues. In the full subconscious awareness that he could never love me back – perhaps, thus proving the case that I am unlovable. I don't believe I am unlovable, but I do feel safer being the person who loves rather than being loved. Once you become consciously aware of why you do the things you do, it is impossible to keep doing them. That level of awareness even changes the external world and the people you attract into your life.

After coffee with Kate, I started to feel really excited about my new beginning. I had never lived anywhere where I thought I was done moving, a place where I could put down roots. I always knew I would leave London, so I wanted to make sure the place I would move to, would be a place where there would be an amazing job and an even more amazing man.

I had lived in Somerset as a teenager, but had lost touch with every one of my school friends. Bristol had always felt like the 'big smoke' but I had never lived there. I had moved to London instead, but now Bristol feels now like it might have interesting potential. And, as I began to think more about it, so I also think about the importance of being in a place I can feel is home – I think that place is Bristol.

Thursday 5th May

I arrived at the hotel this afternoon; it's dog friendly of course. The ceiling has low-hung beams and you'd have to be the height of a dog not to bang your head on the ceiling. The floor also has an uneven surface, so even if you're not drunk, you feel drunk. If I had been drunk, I might not have been so close to cracking my head. I stood at the side of the bed for a moment and did that thinking thing when your mind is full of nothing. Like that moment when you walk into a room and try and remember what you went in there for. Here I was in Bristol and I had strangely forgotten what I had come here for.

Aha yes, it came to me. I had come to Bristol for a life! If this is to be my home, I have two days to find somewhere to live. It all felt a little bit nuts, but if something is meant to be, it will be, or at least that's what you tell yourself to stop the inner-control monkey freaking out that you seriously do not have a plan!

Of course, I picked the most expensive area of the city to check out. I didn't have much of an idea where I was, so I stepped out of the hotel, the dog took a left and I followed. Large Victorian properties and part of the university, I liked what I was seeing. As I walked I found a DVD rental place. Low-beamed ceilings again and a floor that seemed to bow. I loved it, and it just like the one in

San Francisco with a great choice of documentaries as well as recent films. The guy behind the counter was really friendly. He had a cherub face that didn't stop grinning and like me he was a sci-fi fan.

'No dog treats,' I exclaimed on the way out to the dog, who looked genuinely disappointed. I found a pathway with two stretches of park on either side and let her off the lead. Couples were out arm in arm and, even though it was a quiet evening, the place had a buzz about it.

I sat on the wall and watched the dog chase the squirrels. It seemed to me that the squirrels had sized her up as no real threat and couldn't really be bothered to run away from her until the very last second. Straight up a tree, shaking their tails in disgust for having been disturbed. It's the only time you will ever see my dog run, she is the laziest creature and she has never really played with other dogs. A dog analyst said it's because I play with her so often, she doesn't need to run the risk of meeting dogs and playing new games with them. She feels safer with what she knows. They say that dogs are like their owners!

We carried on walking until we came to a delicatessen with a room stretching over the top of the pathway. Outside there were tables and some cute boutiques. That was it! I was suddenly sold. I could see myself living here. The people I would meet, which would be my favourite place to eat. I could see my life here and this being home. I felt really at peace with the moment. I knew there was a long way to go, but it felt good to have decided where to put some roots down.

Friday 6th May

Today I went to a coffee shop with the dog (she was allowed inside, another massive sales point for the area). I got out my laptop and started looking for garden flats. Each call I made, I was told, 'No dogs, No dogs, No dogs'. So I took the dog and walked into an estate agent.

The women at the desk squeaked, 'Oh what a beautiful dog, boy or girl, what breed is she, how old, how long have you had her, she's so adorable!'

'This dog needs a home!' I said and was met with sad eyes from the women, as she obviously thought I was on my way to Battersea Dogs Home or something.

One of the agents told me that it's not the landlords that don't want the dogs but are advised by the estate agents to say, 'No pets'. The sad puppy eyes worked, mine rather than the dog's, and we were given two viewings. One of the places had just become available and already had a dog living there. My appointment was at 5 p.m. and I was really excited. Moreover, I had a good feeling about it.

The first place I saw was no good, done out for renting with a horrible nylon carpet and magnolia walls. I sat in the local pub with the dog to kill the time between viewings. I was shocked to find people actually talked to me as I sat on my own. Not guys in a pub hitting on you, but just people making conversation. Sometimes about the dog, but soon I got them talking about the area and Bristol. I could hear the pride in what the people were saying about the city. I had only really found that before in US, the Brits are often happier to slag off where they live than try and improve it.

While we're on the subject, I have a problem with the word 'they' in context of 'why don't they do something about it...' When you ask those people who 'they' are, they often don't know. It's the council or the government. In my experience that's just giving your power away. In other words, if you're sitting in a bath of poop, don't wait for the bath to be emptied by someone else, get out of the bath!

It was in fact the bath that sold me the flat when I finally got to see it. I viewed the bedroom first, which wasn't a bad size, and then I saw the bathroom. It was the most perfect room ever. I have always dreamed about having a bathroom like the ones you get in five-star hotels, and this was just like that. Separate bath and shower and just a lovely space. I turned to the estate agent and said, 'I'll take it.'

'But you haven't seen the rest of the flat yet,' the estate agent exclaimed.

I didn't need too. I manifested that bathroom. This was my flat. Turned out the rest of the rooms were fine too. I set a date to move in a week later. When things move quickly into place, I psychologically tell myself this is what is meant to happen. Like some unknown force is guiding my hand and when life flows quickly in the right direction, I get the feeling that this unknown force is rewarding me for being an especially good person. When things go wrong, I am being tested for something important. I know on paper this is likely to be a spiritual delusion, however, it is a perk of being an optimist, I can spin anything into a positive.

I have had such a surge of energy about finding a new home, so all of the logistics felt like they would just need a bit of working out, but I'm sure now that everything is going to work out brilliantly.

Monday 8th August

The hardest thing about moving to a place where you don't know anyone is that you don't know anyone! Over the past few months it has felt like a race against time to get my life sorted out. Of course, there is no race and things take as long as they take, but I need to be 'established'. The sooner I can prove everything is working, the sooner I can put the US behind me and the less likely the feeling I have made a big mistake will hit me smack in the face.

So I've been doing my best to stay off Facebook and checking for updates from my previous life, which includes Jax. There has to be a strategy for someone like me who isn't going to get a job and therefore won't be making friends with the people I work with. I decided to use meetup.com and start my own meet-up group. Of course, it's not the same kind of meet-up as the dive bar meet-up group in San Francisco. But I knew that meet-up would be one way of meeting people, getting students/ clients and making a bit of cash. So I pulled all of those strands together and set up one group online called Bristol Socials. My plan: to start an open meet-up group and move towards being together people who wanted to meet people by joining different activities. Of course, the people who really want to meet people are people who have just moved into an area, like me and other single people.

So it's been a great way of finding potential clients.

Meet-up gives you three meet-up groups for the same monthly price. So the next group I set up was called Bristol Social Singles. However, I noticed that the same people are joining both groups, and I really wanted to attract people who aren't on meet-up or who haven't heard of it. So I put flyers in all the cafés for my meet-up group and for my coaching. The other thing that hasn't happened that I know would make a new life easier would be what Nat and I were chasing in San Francisco – the dreaded boyfriend. Yet again the stigma of being a single relationship coach is not a good one.

One woman who's been coming along to my meet-up group is called Karen. She's only recently moved to the Bristol area with her husband for his job. They relocated from London in the big BBC shift that happened. She doesn't have any friends here and she's a stay-at-home mum, so finds it hard to meet people. There is something slightly manic about her. For example, she laughs at inappropriate times during a conversation.

At first, when we were on our own, I'd often check what I'd just said to see what she'd found funny but couldn't place it. I thought there was something odd about me and perhaps I was saying some words with a slight American lilt that she found funny. But the same thing happened when we were in a group too, and so now I've decided that she must have a form of laughter Tourette's, so instead of swearing, she just giggles and sometimes says, 'Yer' or 'Right'.

Of course, as soon as I realised that her laugh was unrelated to anything actually happening I found her addictively adorable. So now, Karen and I often meet for coffee and she tells me about her kids and her husband's job, but not about her husband. She knows so much about his job; she could do it for him. It makes me think how solidly boring their relationship must be, as he must be talking about work all the time for her to be such an expert.

The other thing is that, because this is her life, she also doesn't have much to talk to me about. And so our conversation subjects are becoming more and more diverse from talking about Enneagram personality tests through to whether they've really landed astronauts on the moon or not, as the flag was blowing and there is no wind on the moon. Most of the time, Karen just laughs and nods in response or says, 'Yer, right' as if she already knows everything I am talking about.

A couple of weeks ago, however, she surprised me. Suddenly from out of nowhere she said, 'I want to go dancing.'

How could I refuse?

Thursday 11th August

Tonight was my big night out with Karen. We decided to go to Reflex, a 1980s music-based club in the centre of town. She doesn't have much money so we had some wine at my place before going out. We were horribly early and the bouncers wouldn't let us in. They said the club didn't open until 10 p.m. and didn't really get going until about midnight. That felt late for us, as we didn't plan being out later than 1 a.m. So, we went to the bar next door but it wasn't long before the horrible sense of 'are we too old for this' started to creep down.

We sat a while in silence and looked at our drinks. I wanted to get the *va va voom* going, mostly for her, as I knew this was a rare occasion for her to get away from the kids. So while she checked her phone for incoming calls from her husband with a child-pooping crisis, I decided we should play pool.

Pool is one of those games I used to love, never very good at it, but the point wasn't popping balls down a hole, the point was to angle your bend over the table in a direct line to the guy you fancied so he would get an eyeful of your ample backside. I had forgotten this was what I liked about the game, and now my ample backside seemed to have moved sideways and become ample hips too. I was trying to hit the ball with the cue by curtsying by the side of the table rather than sticking my ass in the air.

A girl on the table next to us was wearing a white mini skirt and white stilettos, with fake-tanned brown legs. Even if I were in a push-up bra with 'Hello Boys' written on my breasts I wouldn't have got any attention next to her. However, the guys who had their eyes pinned to her cheeks were not my kind of guys. We left for Reflex but once inside we realised we were the only two people in there. The bar fridges were full of drinks I didn't recognise and which looked like they might possibly be radioactive.

Some women started to arrive who looked as if they were all on a hen night. All dressed up in outfits that must have looked great in when they bought them, but that was twenty years ago and things had changed! We were simply too sober for this evening, so I bought some shots in order to make it bearable. Pretty soon we were dancing to Adam Ant and doing air whipping to 'Prince Charming', and sticking a pose to Madonna. The whole thing became a play act re-creating the pop videos of the 1980s. I then looked up and realised that the upper ring around the dance floor was full of men watching, and what every other woman was doing was showing off their arse-ettes to the sweating balding onlookers.

Then, from out of nowhere, in a haze of fresh testosterone came the boys, a flock of T-shirts and jeans came to the floor and began to dance. The women scattered in all directions, handbags kicked to the outer reaches of the dance floor and suddenly we were in the middle surrounded by young fit boys! Boys who knew the words to Frankie Goes To Hollywood. I tried to relax but I was tripping off the excitement. Suddenly there was an audience for my impressions of Simon Le Bon. Up to this point it was only Karen who was laughing and let's face it Karen would laugh at anything! Karen's purse was in my bag, so she took my bag to the bar to get some more drinks. While she was gone a lad started dancing with me. I thought this was sweet as I was on my own, he was funny and we were messing around together. He decided to show off and do a bit of pole dancing on a golden pole that ran down the side of the DJ's decks.

Now I have seen drunk guys try this on YouTube and it doesn't go well, so as he took hold of the pole I almost closed my eyes and winced on his behalf. It was as if the whole nightclub held its breath for the impending disaster. Instead he spun round the pole perfectly, and then turned upside-down and wrapped his legs round it. His shirt fell over his face revealing his chest up to his nipples; he sat himself up on the pole using only his abs. I was impressed! He then slid down the pole looking at me.

'That was amazing,' I said.

'Ex-gymnast,' he said and I felt my pussy start to tighten!

Looking at him, I thought me might be about Jax's age. Not as good looking as Jax, but well-defined arms and pecs with a little bit of a tummy on him, but I don't mind that. As I paid him attention and danced with him, his much better looking friend decided to block his chances with me by dancing with me and cutting him off with his body. It was so obvious to me that the good-looking one, who looked like Tom Cruise when he was in *Cocktail*, had no interest in me. But he wanted me to have interest in him, so I would ditch dancing with his mate and his mate would be snubbed. I could tell he must have done this a thousand times before. So I turned to the guy who had been dancing with me first off and put my arms around his shoulders, blocking Tom Cruise out of the picture.

I felt the shock come from the gallery above, as the bald fat guys were now watching the cougars pick off the cubs. Karen came back with the drinks and didn't know where to put herself or the drinks. So I peeled myself off the guy and planted a kiss on his cheek. His aftershave was strong and I knew I would be able to smell it on my top lip for the rest of the evening. His mate stood very still as if in shock as I threw him my best sideways sexy 'you want it, but you're just not gonna get it!' look.

His friend asked for my number and I simply said, 'Phone,' and plugged myself into his contact list.

The ladies had left the dance floor! And after a swig of the most revolting white wine, the ladies left the club too!

On the bus on the way home my phone pinged. It was the Gym Puppy asking when we could meet. I then felt a bit sorry for him, as I had no intention of meeting him. I sent him a text back.

It was lovely to meet you, but I think I'm a bit too old for you. Sam x

Only a few years, why how old are you?

How old are you?

Turned twenty-three last month.

Well add fifteen years to that and you're in my ballpark.

No way do you look 38!

Thanks.

Well can't an older lady be taken out to dinner and have a nice evening?

OK, dark restaurant and you're paying. Sam x

You're on! x

Well I didn't expect that! Bristol was getting more interesting by the minute. I think I'd shocked Karen. She's been married for a long time and was worried about the dangers of me meeting up with a man I don't know. But everyone you meet starts off as being someone you don't know!

'I was really scared about coming to the meet-up group,' she told me. Apparently, she had stood standing outside shaking before deciding to come into the pub. 'If there hadn't been an obvious "meet-up" sign on the table, I would have walked right out the door.' She then laughed as if that would have been crazy, like dancing in nipple tassels in Marks and Spencer's.

'You could have always asked the bartender.'

'Oh God No! My husband said it would do me good to get out more and meet people.'

'Well it sounds like it's been good for you.'

'Yes it has,' she replied.

I have never seen myself as being confident, but in the company of someone with no confidence I must look like an excited Labrador standing next to a shivering Chihuahua. It was at that moment that I started to wonder whether our friendship had any legs or if my over-exuberance would put her off.

I wouldn't dare tell her about Jax and never about the sex club! The more life experience you have, the less you can share, and so the more alone you feel. You would think the more you do, the more you have in common with people – but you also become fragmented, so you become different people with different people. Get them all in the same room and you look like a chameleon with a disco ball shoved up your backside.

Saturday 13th August

Turns out that Gym Puppy is called Jon. We met last night at Las Iguanas, as I still had the image of a chameleon with a disco ball in my head. He's a sweet kid, and spilled an interesting life story out to me over dinner. He has ADHD but did a very good job at following our conversation. He just seemed to have a hard time keeping still.

He told me that when his parents split up he had gone to live with his dad, as his mum couldn't handle both him and his brother. When his dad met someone else, she already had three kids and they all lived together. His new step-mum also couldn't handle him and fights would break out between him and his new step-siblings. So they made him a bedroom in the shed, very Harry Potter. He had shelves and a heater, but it was damp and, well, a shed! He was also scared of the dark, so the sounds of foxes outside or any other nighttime noises meant he didn't sleep well. He hadn't told his dad because he was worried he would be put into care. He'd failed all of his school exams and now works for the Post Office. I felt really heartbroken for him.

To lighten the subject, I asked him what he likes in a girl, does he have a 'type'. He said his last girlfriend was forty-one and from Thailand. Another massive age gap! I could see there was a longing for a mother type. Her family brings people over from Thailand who wanted to live in the UK. They were very rich, as people paid them big sums to come over and she would get them settled in this country. She was the boss of a number of massage parlours. It sounded like people trafficking to me, and the hairs on the back of my neck were standing on end, but he sounded so innocent when he described how much she was helping people.

She had told him she had gone on the pill, which became an obvious lie when she became pregnant. She left him before the baby was born and went back to Thailand. He knows he had a girl but has no idea what she looks like. Then he began to cry. He was drinking the wine much faster than me, but at this point he started gulping. My heart bled for him. We women have some hard stuff to deal with from our male counterparts, but a switch has happened in our society and I think men have it much harder when it comes to being out of control as a dad. I said some kind words and we talked a while. I paid for my half of the dinner and then paid a cab driver to take him home as he was too sloshed to take a bus by the time we said good night.

Later that night I had another dream about Mark. This time we were on the ferry in San Francisco Bay heading towards Alcatraz. We had decided that we were going to have sex in one of the cells. Mark was wearing sunglasses and I was getting frustrated that he seemed uninterested and kept looking out over the harbour between the bridges. So I told him about my recurring dream and how in the dream we are going to have sex, but then we never do.

'You were always been a bit weird,' he said.

Then I woke up. I have no idea what these dreams mean. Of course, I think we are going to a prison, so it might be a subconscious belief that all relationships imprison you. But that's too obvious. In every dream he is disinterested in me, so maybe it is about self-love/self-esteem as Nat said. My number one annoyance is that I didn't get to sleep with him in life and now I don't get to sleep with him night after night! I wonder if the only way to make them stop is to sleep with him.

This morning I looked for him on Facebook but there was no sniff of a profile for him. I guess I need to lucid dream and change the ending!

Saturday 20th August

Karen told me she wants to go out more, so we checked out the speakeasy bars of Bristol tonight. There are three of them and they are low-lit bars, which I love. To gain admission you have to knock on the door and be viewed through a peephole before they decide whether or not they'll let you in. The idea comes from the speakeasy in the days of prohibition in America when alcohol was illegal and a password was needed to get into the places where you could drink. From the outside it doesn't look much like a bar, and the drinks are also expensive.

I was hoping all of the above would be a deterrent for Bristol's students. Not that there is anything wrong with students, but they are often called things like Tarquin, Olivia, Giles, Piers or Edward, I know this because they scream to each other outside the window of my flat in Clifton – 'Giles, I think I've urinated in my Kelvins.'

I know at their age I was oblivious to anyone else in the world too, but it doesn't stop me wanting to kill them at 3 a.m. when the dog is barking at them!

We decided to try the one near the Clifton Triangle called the Hyde Bar. We were let in with no problem at all. Karen loved it, but then she was talking in quite a loud voice, as if we didn't belong in there, and starting saying things like, 'It's really posh isn't it? It's a bit expensive.'

I'm very good at blending wherever I go and often give the impression of being middle-class, when the opposite is true. As a child, I lived in a block of flats that were so ropey they made a documentary about them. But still I was cringing a bit as people turned to look at her. I made the excuse of it being too expensive and we moved on to the Magic Bar.

There was a guy singing along to the piano and some of the other customers were joining in. Somehow, even en masse, most people can sing Robbie William's song 'Angels' in harmony. I think Robbie should write football anthems that get sung during games. I think he could make football fans sound like a choir.

Karen wanted to go dancing, so after a few more rounds of singalong a Robbie and Coldplay, we found a club called La Rocca. Inside it was really small, but the bar staff were friendly and the drinks didn't glow in the dark. Karen put her money in my bag; we put everything else in the cloakroom and hit the dance floor. There was a whole range of age groups there, so it didn't feel like granny fest. The music was a bit cheesy, but we had come to terms with the fact that if you want cool you have to be at a different kind of club, a club where the cool people go and that wasn't us. Karen knocked back her drink and she already had more than her usual quota when we got here. A guy came over and started dancing with us. He seemed nice but a bit dim, however, Karen was all over him.

I left them and went to the bathroom, and when I came back Karen looked happy enough so I went for a walk around to see what there was of the place. Mostly two rooms made to look bigger with mirrors. I got talking to a guy at the bar that works in television so I jumped on him to talk about my book. Karen came over, as she needed my bag to buy drinks. I have the TV guy pinned to the bar in conversation and left Karen with the bag. Once his ears had turned brown and his girlfriend came over I went looking for Karen. I found her at the bar doing shots with nice but dim and a few others. I was introduced to Tarquin, Roger and Ed – *You have got to be kidding me*! Karen was looking drunk, then 'Prince Charming' came on and she started air whipping in the bar.

Somehow air whipping in a bar looks totally different from air whipping on a dance floor, mostly because you can't hear the song as well or get the reference. Back on the dance floor, Karen was reverse parking her backside onto Tarquin's crotch. Ed was trying to dance with me, but looked ungainly as if he really had to think about tipping to the right, then tipping to the left. I went off for another wander around and a people watch.

When I came back Karen was pinned up against the wall being snogged by Tarquin. It was obvious to anyone with eyes who might be looking that his hand was under her skirt and he was rubbing her clit on the outside of her thick tights. Her face was reminiscent of how the girl in the sex club looked when my hand was underneath her dress. Her hand was rubbing his cock over his chinos, I knew she would regret this in the morning, but I could tell this was something she really needed, and then I suddenly realised what was wrong with Karen, why the silly laugh and the nervous disposition. She wasn't getting any sex!

Well maybe her husband after all this time would still give her one after bath time on a Sunday night. But I mean that knee-wobbling desire where you feel like you're going to die unless you get him inside of you. There is nothing more fulfilling than truly wonderful sex. It just takes a good hard cock and someone who takes the time to allow your body to open at their fingertips. Devouring, hot, passionate sex, the kind of sex that leaves your body drenched in relaxation. I could see on Karen's face, which was partly obscured by Tarquin's that she wanted it. I had to go over to get my handbag, which contained my keys, money and phone. Karen asked if she and Tarquin could come back to my place.

In my one-bedroom flat that was going to be difficult and I wasn't sure I wanted to be the person who had helped her to cheat on her husband. However, I knew that look, and she was safer coming home with me than going back to his place, and I knew this was important to her.

'I'm only fooling around,' she said, 'I'm not going to do it.' But I think we both know she was kidding herself.

The taxi ride back was almost silent. Tarquin started talking to me as if he was twelve and I was the mum of his best friend along the lines of, 'Very nice of you to let us come back to your place, Mrs Sam.'

I just hoped I wouldn't get a 'Thank you for having me' in the morning.

When we got out of the taxi I went to pay and discovered that I didn't have the cash I thought I had. It seemed that Karen's £20 had gone a whole lot further than she had thought. In fact she spent it and had gone on to spend my money too thinking it was hers. Tarquin paid for the taxi. Karen thought spending my money was funny but then she was pissed.

In the flat I opened a bottle of wine for them and showed them how to pull out the sofa into a bed then disappeared with the dog into my bedroom. It wasn't long before I could hear the sounds of sex going on in the other room. Something about hearing other people have sex ether makes you feel horny or lonely. This one was lonely, I thought about Jax, Nat, Anna and San Francisco. I thought that really my life coming back to the UK hadn't changed that much. There is a saying, 'Where ever you go, there you are!'

In the morning Tarquin had gone by the time I got up. My dog barked his departure out of the door. I waited until I heard Karen go to the bathroom before offering her tea. She looked shell shocked.

'How was it?' I asked her.

'Really good,' she said. 'Just what I needed, and the last thing I need.' She looked like she had softened, looked younger. If it hadn't been for the look of fear in her eyes, she would also have looked calmer. Then she said from out of nowhere, 'He came on my face.'

'I hope he had the decency to wipe it off.'

'No, it was very porn star like, he wanted me to stick my tongue out.'

God only knows if Karen has ever really seen a porn film or is guessing at this point.

'I didn't like it,' she said. 'It's like someone spitting in your face, it's so impersonal. Can I have a shower in case it's in my hair still?'

'Of course.'

I understood completely what she meant, she wanted the great desire and lust with crazy sex, yet it to be with someone who respected her. The act of splashing cum on her face had turned her from a person into an object. Different if it's anywhere else on the body and he has to clean it up, otherwise his act turns you into a slut. It's never the action; it's always the intention behind it. I realised this was true also in the faked condom I had experienced with Dean. We decided to keep the whole episode a secret as we said goodbye and Karen returned to her husband.

But I know I won't see her again. It's really hard to look in the face of the person who reminds you of your guilt – but last night probably saved her marriage or at least given it another five years.

Thursday 25th August

Cash flow hasn't been coming in fast enough for the rent – I knew it would be a stretch to pay for this flat before building my business in the area, but at least I have the dwindling savings from my house sale to fall back on if necessary. So, I've decided to put a profile up on LinkedIn and see what happens. It might be a way to get a job, even in the short term, while I build everything up.

It's taken me two days to get my profile right, which I spent sitting on the floor going through all my old diaries, trying to put together all my work history dates. Although most of it seems irrelevant since I've been working for myself for so long. Today, I finished it, and immediately started to look for other people I know. Of course, as soon as the thought 'find people I know' popped into my head so did Mark!

Mark, the man of my dreams, literally my dreams! I was disappointed when he didn't pop up on Facebook a few days ago when I'd tried and it's been twenty-three years since I have seen him outside of a dream. So, I wasn't expecting a lot when I searched for his name. But then a profile popped up without a picture.

Thinking, it couldn't be him because that would be way too easy, I clicked on the profile and it opened. Immediately some key words jumped out at me, which matched the odd bits of information I had heard from people I went to school with…this was totally his profile. I had found him and I froze as if I had just been caught hacking into a boyfriend's emails, and discovered a stash of lesbian porn. I was intrigued and terrified all at the same time. Little did I know that LinkedIn tells you who has viewed your profile!

I pondered what to do. Did I have the audacity to send him an email? What would I say: 'How are you? I keep having these crazy dreams in which we are about to have sex but we never do, and then in the dream I tell you that I have been having these crazy dreams!'

I laughed at myself and decided it was a bit of a hopeless situation unless I was going to get some balls. Not enough balls to contact him, I had those, but the kind of resilient balls I would need when his rejection, lack of contact, sudden closure of his LinkedIn account, email comprising the words 'fuck off' or whatever emotional device would be used to cut off the aforementioned balls. I would need them to be made of steel or bombproof concrete.

Mark has travelled with me in my dreams for twenty-three years. If I were to contact him after all this time and nothing were to happen…there is nothing I would hate more than nothing. Nothing is very likely, and he might not even remember who I am. He maybe still married, five kids, or fat and bald or gay! I also didn't know what I wanted, well I wanted to know what the dreams were all about, but he wouldn't know. Unless he was having them too and then that would be totally mental. I just didn't know the guy, so how would I know what I wanted. Holding a torch for someone for that long isn't romantic it's tragic, and if it weren't for the dreams then I wouldn't even be looking.

OK that's not true, if he were on Facebook I would be looking to see if he was fat/bald and how beautiful his wife was.

Still pondering I looked at Jax's Facebook account. There wasn't any new news, everything seemed the same, but my feelings about him had changed. I didn't feel that sense of responsibility for him. I had closed that window.

I logged out of Facebook and was pleased to see that I already had a notification from LinkedIn.

Mark Nicholson has viewed your profile.

Mark Nicholson...Mark Nicholson...Mark Nicholson... Mark...fuck me...Nicholson!

I had to read the words a few times because his name is only in my head, never on paper and here it was on the screen in a place it's not supposed to be. Mark Nicholson in my awake-time and in my inbox. I freaked out! I soon twigged that Mark must have got the same email, when I viewed his profile.

Names become icons and seeing his name in my inbox after searching for a mention of him for so long, seemed completely out of place. Just his name, the identity of someone you know from the past but don't know anymore and the one unchanged factor, his name.

I grabbed the dog lead and we took a long walk over the downs to where I could see the water below and the Clifton Suspension Bridge in the distance. There are a lot of similarities between Bristol and San Francisco. I would have loved to call Nat and tell her what had just happened, or wander into the kitchen to see if Anna was in there. Looking across the downs and the space around me, I relaxed and allowed the air to fill my lungs instead of the shallow breathing I had been doing since receiving the notification from LinkedIn. In doing so, I decided there was nothing to be done. He knows I have stroked his profile. He will send me an email or he won't, but I can't send him one, I don't have the balls.

I walked back to the flat and took a shower before checking my emails, so my hair wasn't remotely dry when I did check – nothing there. I got dressed and dried my hair, came back to the PC, nothing there. I closed my eyes and took a breath. OK, it's OK. It's likely better this way, I opened my eyes and there was an email. I looked harder, read the name five times. It was really him.

His email read:

> Wow, now there's a name from way back! When LinkedIn messaged to say you had visited my profile it was quite a shock – in a nice way obviously!
>
> I did start to work out how long it has been but gave up as it started to make me feel old… :-)
>
> So how are you?
>
> Mark

So I did what any normal person would do…I cleaned the kitchen.

I did consider continuing on to the bathroom, but I now knew what I wanted to say back and enough time had passed (the kitchen was a mess) for me to reply without looking desperate.

I randomly bumped into you in the street in London in 1995/6. I can remember what job I was doing, so the year is easy to come up with. I'm not working out how old I was, or I really will start to feel old!

Thanks for emailing, it's great to hear from you.

I'm well, happy and all the things you could hope for :) Returned to the West Country after living in San Francisco. I'm an author and yoga teacher, live with a super cute dog.

How about you? What did you do with your life? That is quite a ridiculous question but sums up the thousand little questions I would love to ask you. I'm terribly curious, which is what got me so busted on LinkedIn!

So hello, Mark, who are you now? :)

Sam

(Skipped saying I'm a love coach!)
He wrote back right away...OK so when he does it, it's sweet. When I do it, it's desperate!

'Who are you now?' Jeez can you start with an easier question?! ;-)

An author eh? Congratulations! I'm impressed.

Was it 1995/6? God that feels a lifetime ago, let's agree never to mention dates again!

If I gave you the full version I'm sure you could use your author skills to sell it to Eastenders :-) I'm divorced have one kid, Ben who is the light of my life and I have him 50 per cent of the week split with my ex.

So you're in Bristol? We should meet up, as your 999 other questions will take ages by email ;-) Plus I'm really intrigued to find out more about what you're up to now.

Mark

OMG OMG OMG OMG OMG OMG OMG OMG
OMG OMG OMG OMG OMG OMG OMG OMG
OMG OMG OMG OMG OMG OMG OMG OMG
OMG OMG OMG OMG OMG OMG OMG OMG
    Fuck!

Cleaned the bathroom! While bending over the bath, I suddenly remembered I had written about him in my book. As I never really expected to see him again, I never expected he would read it. I talked about something that had happened one day at the beach and how I had wished he had been the guy I gave my virginity to in that moment. That's quite a way to admit something like that! I might now finally get to the bottom of the dream. That is going to be the weirdest moment, when I tell him about the dream; it will be like I'm dreaming. The whole of this feels a bit surreal already. I wrote:

Wow! Sounds like you have had a few bruises in that time! I look forward to the full version when I see you, or just the edited film trailer so I can get my pitch to the

TV companies right ;) You have been immortalised in my book, not by name of course, just something that happened when I was with you once. I'll give you a copy of the book with your part underlined :)

I am in Bristol. LinkedIn said you're in Cheltenham? Not massively far away if so. Let me know your timetable and we can get something together. It would be great to see you and try to fill in 'an undisclosed never to be mentioned again', amount of time! :)

His reply came swiftly again:

Bruised is definitely a good word to describe it all…

I've just ordered your book, as I am concerned that I'm in there!!!

I could do Monday, Tuesday or Friday next week if you're free?

So what kind of dog and what's it called?

Mark

Changed the sheets in the bedroom! No, not because I think I might get lucky, but because this is all moving a bit too fast! After twenty-three years of wondering about him, I could see him on Monday! It seems almost too easy! I feel like a hole has been blown open in my limited universe and suddenly everything seems possible, and rather than this being an amazing feeling of unlimited manifestation, I'm bricking it! Of course I want to meet him and I totally will but I just feel like I am suddenly living at altitude and there is a wind blowing through my brain!

We make an arrangement to meet on Tuesday. I think the Hyde Bar is the best place; it's dark quite perfect, apart from being a sod to find! So, I am going to meet Mark outside Browns instead and take him over to the Hyde Bar. He also really likes the sound of the Hyde Bar, so I think I may have scored myself a sophistication brownie point.

Tuesday 30th August

I was early. I am always early. Standing at the top of the steps, I had a vantage point and would be able to see him coming up the steps towards me. I don't know if he has changed much. I'm trying not to read into his keenness to see me. My head is jumping between 'he really wants a relationship' or 'he's hit a few branches on the ugly tree falling out of his marriage and I have out-aged him in hotness!' I'm trying to keep the whole thing very simple and not making meaning out of stuff. Such a typical thing us women do.

As it got towards 7 p.m. the time we were due to meet, I started to relax. I felt this flow of calm start to come though me, and this just felt like a fixed point in time – something meant to me – and if I totally screwed it up then I was meant to screw it up. From that realisation, I breathed out, as if I were mediating. I felt totally in the moment, right here, right now!

Then a hand was placed on my shoulder from behind, I jumped out of my skin right into Mark's chest. I could smell him before I looked into his eyes. His smell was intoxicating and kind of familiar, and I felt myself wobble a little. I had forgotten how tall he was, and it seemed to take forever for my head to slowly tip back to look into his eyes. He wasn't looking at me.

'Hello, Sam,' he said.

I looked into his face and saw he had a few laughter lines around his eyes, but he hadn't changed much – wasn't fat and still had all his hair. In fact he looked exactly like he does in my dreams. He was early so he had gone to get a drink inside to calm his nerves, while I was early and waiting outside for him, so my vantage point was never going to work. I couldn't take my eyes off his face; I kept morphing it with the face of the young boy I had known. He was most definitely all man now. He even had the vibe of being a dad. He couldn't look me in the eye and I couldn't stop talking absolute shite!

We crossed the road towards the Hyde Bar and I didn't even see the traffic, he touched my arm at one point, as I was about to send a student on a bike flying across the road. It seemed to take a dog's age standing outside the bar waiting for them to let us in. I was on the top step and he the one below, so when he turned and looked into my eyes for the first time it was at eye level. In that very moment, I felt at peace, like I had come home.

'They have seen you, and they not going to let us in,' Mark smirked.

'Must be after that table dancing last time,' I quipped back.

'Oh not again, thought you would have given that up by now,' Mark said.

The door opened and we were led to a table.

Talking to him felt like sitting in confessional. I told him everything about my life, and I listened as his story unfolded. I remember Nat saying that the right guy would accept you and your past for who you really are. I didn't believe her and yet here was I telling Mark everything, like

I couldn't hold back my honesty. I could hear the words I was saying out loud and I was finding it surprising that I felt so comfortable just being myself. I told him about the extent of the crush I had on him at school, that I had stayed on in sixth form because he was and I told him about the sex club in San Francisco.

'It sounds like you have had a very big life,' he said

I looked for a tone of judgement in what he said; I couldn't find one so I asked him, 'In a bad way?'

'Not at all, you were always the same at school, everyone else was small minded and looking inside the school gates, gossiping and looking at what they would do with their lives from what they knew. You were terrifying. You kept pointing to the windows and saying 'look outside everyone there's a big world out there'. It's what I liked about you and why I couldn't have dated you. Your perspective on life is just massive. You scared everyone because most people don't want to see a big picture. Now I am on the other side of my marriage, I just want the big picture. It doesn't surprise me at all that you have done all of that stuff. Life just never seemed to be enough for you, you always wanted more.'

It was such a relief to be accepted. But I also started to realise where I had been going wrong in relationships. It really never has been enough for me, so how would any man feel like he could be enough for me. I would have to reach a point of self-acceptance, which I knew was the thing lacking and making me want to be enough, by absorbing more and more life experiences.

It was a rich and intense exchange, anyone watching us would have wondered if we were planning a robbery. I was aware of the table behind me because someone kept banging the table, like table drumming but not in time to anything. I could feel their energy boring into my back as if they wanted to get my attention. I put up an intention force field around me, so I could block them out and listen fully to Mark. A peanut missile came over my head and onto the table. We also had a bowl of nuts, untouched because eating them would have distracted from our conversation. Twerp Head behind me was also a distraction and one I needed to nip in the bud. Start friendly!

I turned and said, 'We have a whole bowl of nuts over here. I don't think you want to start nut wars with us.' Big smile!

Twerp Head picked up a handful of nuts and chucked them at my face.

I clocked his position. He was sitting on a leather pouffe; his friend was on my left hemmed in a little by the edge of the table. They couldn't see Mark as he was behind a pillar. All this information was relevant because if this next move didn't go well, I knew that I could get from my seated position, onto their table and come down on Twerp Head with my hands round his neck and he'd be on his back on the floor within seconds. Of course, I had no intention of doing this, but knowing you can back up a statement makes the energy behind what you are staying plausible. You believe it, they believe it and then they're less likely to test you on it.

He must have only been about twenty-three. I had waited the whole of his lifetime to meet with the man I was sitting with. The adrenaline from simply meeting Mark was still coursing through my body. I slowly leaned forwards towards his face and let the peanut drop out of my cleavage. Big breasts are powerful when used in the right way, and if not, they make a famously good distraction while kicking someone in the...nuts!

'You don't know me, and you don't want to mess with me, not tonight, not ever.'

'Ooooh! Really!'

'Yes really, you don't know me. You have picked the wrong woman.'

My conviction and the slightly mad look in my eyes was enough to make him wonder what I might have up my sleeve. I have been in places and seen things that would fry his young mind, and I had no intention of letting this little Dick Splash spoil my evening. Looking at him, his face morphed with Jax and I realised they might be about the same age. Jax was emotionally and mentally far superior to this guy. But then I remembered Jax the night after the sex club, how he had just been getting in people's faces. Maybe this guy was just in a total place of frustration in his life. Regardless of where he was, he was in the wrong place in regards to me. As I slowly turned back to Mark, I realised he had heard the whole thing. This isn't what good girls do. Good girls don't turn into the goddess Kali over a cocktail.

As I looked at him, he was smiling, 'You haven't changed,' he said.

The table tapping from behind stopped and so I got to tell Mark about my dream. I had a few false starts in telling him, because telling someone that you dream about nearly having sex with them AND wanting to have sex with them takes some careful phrasing...and I did want to sleep with him. Every time he looked me in the eyes I nearly stopped breathing, which when your halfway through a sentence makes you sound a bit breathy. He smiled when I told him and we pondered upon what the dream was all about. He didn't talk too much about it. He told me at school I was always the weird one.

He wasn't surprised that I hadn't settled down, and made some comment about me blossoming with age, but I didn't quite catch it and it's hard to ask for a repeat of a compliment – especially as the way he said it made me wonder/hope that he was hitting on me. We kept 'accidentally' touching each other, which got easier the more we drank. Every time he so much as brushed me, electric shocks ran through me.

I had totally forgotten about Twerp Head and Dick Splash when I heard one of them shout, 'Oy!'

'Oy!'

'Oy!'

'Oy!'

'Oy!'

I didn't want to do it. I didn't want to break this moment and I didn't want to deal with these little pricks. I suddenly felt vulnerable and exhausted. I had had enough of putting out fires. The past few hours with Mark, had been like finding lost parts of myself. It had been a moving experience and I finally felt less fragmented. Telling my life story to someone who was fully witnessing me and giving me acceptance was so powerful, especially as I had spent a good part of my school life and early twenties trying to get noticed by this guy. Hearing his impressions of me from way back when, made me feel like all this time he did see me. It was me who couldn't see myself and that was what I was looking for in San Francisco. I was looking to accept myself.

'Swap seats,' Mark said.

Genius idea, swapping seats put me behind the pillar so they couldn't see me. Hide in the Hyde Bar, brilliant. But that wasn't what he meant. As we swapped seats, Mark didn't sit down, he towered over the boys. Slowly moving his gaze from one boy to the other with a grimacing look on his face. The boys looked scared. Without saying a word, he lifted his trousers at the knees slightly, sat down and smiled at me. For once in my life, it wasn't me who had to be in control of the situation. I was protected and supported and I had never had that before. Over Mark's shoulder I saw the lads leave.

I didn't want the night to end. I was scared that I was going to go back to who I was before this moment and something had shifted. Something in how I felt about myself had shifted. It wasn't some romantic notion of falling in love with him. I was falling in love with myself in his company. I could see who I really was and my values and place in the world. It was like an out breath, all at one, all is perfect and it is how it is meant to be. As we got ourselves together to leave at the end of the night, I didn't want to let go of his side. I didn't want this to be it and for me never to see him again. I didn't want to go back to my old feeling about me. Like an addict not wanting to feel straight again. Yet at the same time I wanted this to be it, it was so perfect, I didn't want to spoil the memory of the evening by perusing something else with this man, that would likely lead to disappointment and me blowing it up into something it wasn't. I didn't want something to go wrong with our connection, before the new painted me was dry. The best way to break it would be to sleep with him and that would put an end to the dream too. He was kind of a conquest with my dream self, and yet at the same time not sleeping with him was the story. If I slept with him, we were done.

At the bus stop I put my hand on his leg, the indication being, *this is the moment you kiss me!* He tilted his head to one side and looked at me and said, 'Which bus do you need?'

I was suddenly filled with the urgent need to leave. I was way too drunk for this situation and knew I wasn't thinking straight. I pegged it across the road to the taxi rank, not knowing if he was behind me or not. I jumped into a black cab and swished across the leather seat to the opposite side. I left the door open.

Did he cross the road with me? Is he getting in the cab? I couldn't look. I didn't even know if I wanted him to get in. I just knew I needed him to want me as that would make my very young inner self very happy and if he didn't want me, my current self was OK with that. When I looked up he was holding on to the door and saying, 'I'll see you soon, yes?'

I nodded. He closed the door. The taxi sped up and I slipped my ass down the leather seat towards the seat well.

Sometimes you get a download where everything suddenly makes sense. Like someone gave you the instruction manual to your whole life and here you are, fully understanding yourself for the first time. The taxi ride was one of those moments. From being very drunk I was suddenly sober and so crystal clear about who I am. I realised the reason I am single is because it seemed safe, safe to keep moving. I did think I was enough so I had to experience more. The more I experienced the more fragmented I felt. I had never trusted anyone to love me, because love had always been a tool of manipulation in my experience. I didn't want to be vulnerable like that. But there are different levels of softness and opening. Now I see I have always been vulnerable, and that's good, that's human. I can also see the potential of love, openness and vulnerability to be the greatest tool for learning and the greatest gift you can ever give.

How could I deny someone who might want to give that gift to me, unconditionally! I had been seeking love outside of myself, but I knew in that moment that I AM LOVE. Love in its purest form, I am love and love is me. When I removed the blocks I had put up to stop myself seeing who I really am, all I could see was love. I looked at myself with the kind of compassion I could imagine some kind of God having, You silly fool, you were looking for something you had all the time, now your job can only be to go out and give love, and as you do it will come back to you. I had been somehow looking for permission, looking to be good enough, deserving enough, healed enough to be worthy of something I could no longer deny. I am love and so is everybody else.

I was greeted home at the door, my home, by a very excited dog. She is always excited to see me. In fact she is excited to see total strangers, just not in the same way. She can tell who has an open heart or a closed heart. My heart has been closed and I have been lonely. I can see it now; it is impossible to be lonely with an open heart. I lay on the floor with her as tears of joy streamed down my face. I had finally arrived at myself. I could feel the connection with my dog more fully than I had ever felt it before, the carpet under my hands and the wetness of my cheeks.

Beep! Beep!

Loved this evening thank you. But not ready for anything, sorry. I know this is going to sound like a cliché, but it's not you, it's me. Mark x

Some dreams really do come true ;) Of course it's not me, sweetie! I'm amazing. ☺ Sleep well. Sam x

Beep! Beep!

You are! Thank you. Mark x

Who is Rebecca Stone?

Rebecca Stone is the alter ego of a popular self-help author who shall remain nameless. This nameless author was trying to drum up ideas on how to reach her favourite demographic – people who haven't reached their potential and don't know how amazing they are. She has written books on relationships and self-belief; she's even got as far as having a well-known publishing house publish her books. All of this was working well enough, yet she felt she was preaching to people already in the 'church of self-love', and wondered how to reach the people on the outside?

Then *Fifty Shades of Grey* made it to the big time and it hit nameless author in the face like a slapped arse. As the cries and screams of 'It's not fair!' came from her bedroom, she realised this book WAS reaching...well everyone!

An idea sparked, what if there was a fiction book that allows people to witness a journey to self-love stopping off at some steamy erotic sex along the way...And, so *Cupcakes and Coffee* was born.

A story that takes Sam, who doesn't know she is seeking self-love to an inner place where she finds it. Slip in a few penises, some light-hearted humour and everyone's laughing!

If *Fifty Shades of Grey* met *Bridget Jones* and had

an *Eat Pray Love* child, then you'd meet *Cupcakes and Coffee* for a fearless sexual adventurer.

But wait...wouldn't this confuse nameless' brand and have people thinking this was an autobiographical book? Possibly, so alter ego Rebecca Stone wrote the book on nameless' behalf.

It's wrong that there are so many taboos around smuttery, but that's the way it is. Sex sells and if it can be used as a vehicle to deliver an uncover a powerful message to an audience that might not of heard it otherwise, well you can tie me to a chair and call me Stacey, let's just make it happen!

As an archetypal muse Rebecca Stone is powerful, feminine, sensual and provocative. She believes you can see heaven in another person's eyes and feel the universe though sensual touch. She doesn't promote random promiscuous sex, but says you know in a moment what is right and what is not; and you can go with the flow and have some amazing experiences, if you know how to listen to your authentic heart. The world needs more empowered stress-free people who connect to love over fear. Rebecca is on a mission to make that happen.

If you want to contact Rebecca Stone,
she would love to hear from you.
Email her at rebecca@rebeccastone.info
and follow her on Twitter @RStoneINFO.

Lightning Source UK Ltd.
Milton Keynes UK
UKOW04f0721201114

241870UK00001B/8/P